HUSH NOW

BABY

New York Times & USA Today

Bestselling Author

CHERYL

BRADSHAW

First edition July 2014
Copyright © 2014 by Cheryl Bradshaw
Cover Design Copyright 2014 © Indie Designz
Formatting by Bob Houston eBook Formatting
All rights reserved.

ISBN: 1500258970
ISBN-13: 978-1500258979

DEDICATION

To anyone who has ever struggled with infertility. I
empathize.
And to birth mothers who make the heart-wrenching
decision of choosing adoptive parents to raise your baby.
I applaud your courage.

ACKNOWLEDGEMENTS

This book means a lot to me. From the moment I conceived the idea to write it, I knew I'd have to dig deep, facing my own past struggles with infertility in order to bring the characters to life. As I sit here now, finished and ready to start my next novel, I've taken a moment to reflect one last time on *Hush Now Baby* and all the help I received along the way. To my husband, who probably didn't realize how challenging and rewarding it would be to marry a writer. To family and friends for your unwavering support. To Tansy Shelton for your EMT expertise and helpful suggestions. Janet Green (thewordverve) where do I begin? Thanks for everything—your help, your advice, your friendship. You always understand what I'm trying to say, and my work shines because of it. Amy Jirsa-Smith, I appreciate your attention to detail. Bob Houston and Dafeenah Jameel, for excellence in formatting and for making everything beautiful. Crystal Sershen your voice is perfection! To Elizabeth Winick Rubinstein for finally being the right fit and for believing in me. And because every novel needs a great song, "Pictures of You" by The Cure is the theme song of this novel. Onward!

"I laugh because I must not cry, that is all, that is all."

-Abraham Lincoln

CHAPTER 1

Serena Westwood peeled back the quilt atop her four-poster bed and climbed in, reeling the covers over her shivering body until she'd cocooned herself inside. It was early September, and already the frigid fall air crept through the valley, misting it like a damp sheet struggling in the wind.

After a long, noise-filled day, all was still. There was a time when Serena loved the quiet, basked in the gentle, serene calm, but not now. Now she had more than herself to consider. At thirty-nine years old, Serena had almost convinced herself the role of "mother" was meant for everyone *but* her. She'd spent many restless nights in the same bed she relaxed in now, trying to accept the reality that she, and her husband, Jack, would remain childless forever. And yet, here she was, the proud new mother of a sweet baby boy.

Before Finn was born, Jack and Serena had run the gamut, trying everything from artificial insemination to in-vitro fertilization. Nothing took. Her womb, desolate and barren, had rejected it all. When conceiving a baby themselves was out of the question, they turned to surrogacy. Three potential candidates were interviewed. All were rejected. Another round of women were selected. None seemed like the right fit.

On the way home from the market one wintery afternoon, an SUV struck a patch of ice on the road. The vehicle careened into the oncoming lane, sideswiping Serena's Subaru in the process. While waiting for police to arrive, Serena had taken refuge inside the Precious Gift Adoption Agency.

A firm believer in fate, Serena found herself explaining her unsuccessful plight to Teresa Foster, one of the case workers. Teresa was empathetic, her own life experience mirroring much of what Serena herself had endured, but Teresa's attitude was different. In Teresa's mind, infertility had led her to the greatest gift of all—adoption—and she prevailed upon Serena to think of adoption the same way.

One week and several conversations later, Jack and Serena filled out the necessary paperwork. And although Teresa cautioned them at the onset, saying the wait time for a newborn baby could be two years or more, a mere three months passed before a birth mother

selected Serena and Jack as her adoptive p
months later, Finn made his opening debut.

. . .

The faint hum of a stirring baby jolted Serena
awake. She peered at the clock on the nightstand. Four
a.m. It seemed like only minutes had elapsed since she
rested her head on the pillow, and already, it was
feeding time again.

"Mommy's coming, Finn." Her melodic voice
drifted down the hall.

Serena coiled a tattered robe around her body,
cinching it in front of her waist. She picked a few bobby
pins out of the terry-cloth pocket and twisted her long,
blond locks into a bun. She squeezed the lids over her
hazel eyes open and shut a few times, forcing herself
awake.

The frigid chill of the tiles beneath her feet as she
made her way down the hall were a stern reminder to
leave her slippers by her bedroom door next time. She
entered the kitchen, her mind doing most of the work
for her, having memorized her every move. After
performing the same routine night after night,
intelligent thought was no longer required. The bottles
practically made themselves.

Cupping the bottle in her hand, Serena stirred the formula and water together and popped it into the microwave. She watched the hardened plastic revolve around and around on the circular glass tray like a carousel. For a moment, her eyes closed and she found sleep again until Finn's desperate cries grew louder. She was used to the baby fussing, but he'd never been this agitated before.

"Almost there," she called. "Mommy's coming."

Mommy.

She wasn't used to the name. She wondered if she'd ever get used to it.

The microwave dinged. She removed the bottle and dipped her pinkie finger inside, ensuring the formula had heated just right. Perfect. She screwed the lid on and paused. The crying had stopped.

Had he fallen back to sleep?

All was quiet. Too quiet.

Tiptoeing to the other side of the house, she snuck up to the crib. A wave of panic gripped her. There was no baby.

A low, lucid chirp prompted Serena to whip around. She saw nothing at first, but there was something peculiar about the wall opposite her. A dark shadow in the shape of a person blackened its surface.

Her eyes trailed the shadow to its source—the bedroom door. Was someone behind it?

"Who's there?" Her voice trembled.

No response.

Her eyes tore across the lamp-lit room. Armed with nothing but the baby's bottle, she saw no way to defend herself from the assumed attacker. Her mind raced back to a self-defense class she'd taken years earlier, remembering something the instructor had said about fingers being a person's most viable weapon. "Jab them in the eyes," he'd said, lecturing the room full of women on how to handle an intruder. "Fast and with all the force you can muster. Don't think about it. Just do it."

A knot wrenched her gut. "I asked who's there. Show yourself." She thought about adding the word "please," but didn't want to sound weak.

While there was no movement from behind the door, a second faint squeak emitted from Finn's mouth.

"Who are you?" she cried. "Come out. I know you're there."

A man's voice floated throughout the room. He spoke, but not to her. "Hush now." His tone was rugged, yet soothing enough to quiet the child.

The man remained behind the door, toying with Serena. But why? It didn't matter why. Not really.

Whoever he was, he had her baby, and she was done playing his game. She shaped her fingers into a stiff V and surged forward. The man stepped out, anticipating her protective instinct to react. He had the height of a basketball player and the largest hands she'd ever seen. In one hand he held Finn. In the other, a Sig Sauer .45, aimed right at her head.

"Back…up," he demanded. "Now."

Staring down the barrel of a gun, Serena shied away, seeing no alternative than to comply with his demand.

"Why do you have my baby?" she whispered.

He bounced Finn up and down, his eyes never breaking contact with Serena's terrified face. "*My* baby."

He laughed, finding the comment amusing.

A defiant Serena refused to give in any more than necessary. "What do you mean *your* baby?"

A second nervous laugh escaped from the man's lips.

Finn started to cry.

"He's frightened," Serena said. "Let me hold him. Please."

"Can't."

"Please! You're scaring him!"

She attempted to place the bottle on the nightstand.

"Don't!"

"I was just going to—"

"Your hands," he grunted. "Keep them where I can see them."

She wasn't sure whether to hoist them in the air, palms forward, like she was a hostage, or to let them fall to the side. He picked up on her uncertainty.

"Just … cross your arms or something."

In his eyes she detected inner conflict, like he was wrestling with the decision of whether to keep Finn or give him back. Or maybe she had it all wrong. Maybe he was trying to decide whether *she* lived or died. His hands were steady, not sticky and pulsating like hers. Why was he there? What was his motivation? If only she could figure it out, maybe she could save them both.

She tried appealing to his sensitive side, if he had one. "My son's name is Finn. We adopted him a few weeks ago. He's our only—"

"Shut your mouth, lady. I don't care."

Finn squirmed, growing restless in the man's hand.

Without stepping forward, Serena reached her hands out in front of her.

"Don't … move," the man said through gritted teeth.

He crossed in front of Serena, eased Finn back into the crib.

"Thank you."

No response.

"We have a safe," she added. "I'll show you where it is. Okay?"

With the slowest of movements, she put one foot in front of the other, easing her way toward the door.

"You think I'm here to rob you?"

"Aren't you?" she asked, without looking back.

"Lady, if I wanted to rip you off, I would have done it already."

"If you don't want money, what do you want?"

Thoughts swirled around in her mind, each more sinister than the one before. She breathed in, but it made no difference. It felt like all the air to the room had been sucked out. Another thought occurred: *Is he here to rape me? Then why bother with the baby?*

Serena reminisced on how grateful she'd been when her husband switched from days to swing shift at work. The bump in pay allowed them to come up with the adoption money they needed. Now she wished her husband was by her side, wished Jack was here.

Serena wrapped her arms around herself and bowed her head, pointing the way to the master bedroom at the other end of the hall. "Just get it over with … and then I want you to leave."

"I'm sorry about this. Really, I am."

"If you're sorry, don't do this. Just leave."

"Why couldn't you have stayed asleep?"

"Why couldn't I …?" But it was too late.

He aimed the gun at the back of Serena's head and fired.

CHAPTER 2

Fifteen minutes later, across town

The ceiling in my room was gray. Not a milky, washed-out gray. A charcoal gray, like the color of an angry sky right before a thunderstorm. I'd determined this after staring at it for the past three hours. I'd further determined the painter was a greenhorn, having missed three spots about the size of a quarter, making it appear patchy in some places. It bugged me. If I had a brush and the right shade of paint, I would have fixed it myself, even if it *was* almost five in the morning.

The seconds ticked by, but they never tocked, and per my usual, I remained awake, restless, and riddled with this evening's nightly bout of incertitude. What was I even doing here? By *here* I meant in Jackson Hole, Wyoming, in the guest bedroom of a house owned by one of Jackson Hole's finest detectives, Cade McCoy. Cade liked me. I expect it was part of the reason I'd been invited here. Whether or not I returned the sentiment had yet to be determined.

Cade had asked me to drive up for the weekend to celebrate the sale of my house in Park City, Utah. I didn't feel much like celebrating. Officially, I felt like a homeless person, and unofficially, I was one. After several unsuccessful endeavors to map out my life over the last twenty years, I was tired.

I couldn't see my path anymore.

Maybe because there wasn't one.

I hadn't taken on a new case in over six months, instead choosing to lounge around my house in yoga pants and ribbed tank tops, only venturing out to lunch with my friend Maddie in town. I suspected she'd planned the weekly ritual to ensure I got dressed and entered the land of the living once in a while. Either way, it didn't make a bit of difference—or it hadn't—not yet.

I thought if I took some time off, cared for myself for once, somehow I'd be able to sleep again. And I did, at first. It just wasn't the kind of sleep a person welcomed. While Maddie talked about dreams of passionate rendezvous with seductive men she created with her imagination, my dreams were infested with flashes, scenes from my past, things I didn't want to remember, things I tried to forget. All the pain, hurt, and agony rolled up into one hellacious nightmare after another.

I couldn't escape sleep and survive, so as an alternative, I learned to live on very little of it. I watched every single episode of *The Sopranos* followed by every single episode of *Sex and the City*. I lectured Carrie Bradshaw on her relationships that weaved in and out of her life like a revolving door. I talked to the television screen even though it never talked back, and ignored the growing number of voicemails on my phone.

A few weeks ago, a balled-up fist had almost dented my front door. The persistent pounding was meant to get my attention. My house was under contract, so at first I assumed the soon-to-be new owners had dropped by for their third impromptu visit in a month. Imagine my surprise when the obnoxious noisemaker turned out to be my pint-sized spitfire of a grandmother. At the age of eighty-three, she still managed to pull off a pair of skinny jeans and a white fitted V-neck top, which matched nicely with her short, cropped hair.

"What are you doing here?" I asked. "Aren't you supposed to be in—"

Before I'd finished, she blew past me like I hadn't uttered a word. The door slammed shut behind her. Upon hearing her voice, my westie, Lord Berkeley, whom I'd nicknamed Boo, rounded the corner at warp speed. Gran bent down, and Boo leapt into her arms. She cracked a smile—for him, not for me—and stroked his fur for a few moments before sending him on his way.

She positioned her hands on her hips and eyeballed me, wagging a crooked pointer finger in front of my face. Not a good sign. My body tensed, bracing itself for what was about to come next.

"What in the hell is wrong with you?"

Unsure of what response to give, I gave nothing, electing to respect my elder. It made no difference. She wasn't swayed. Her finger was in such close proximity to my face, it tickled the tip of my nose. I sneezed. She frowned.

"Well?" she continued. "Say something. Anything. Don't just stand there."

"Nice to see you too, Gran."

The words I'd voiced sounded like more of a question than a statement, aggravating her even more.

"When's the last time you accepted a job? When's the last time you returned a phone call?" She sized up my attire. "When's the last time you bathed?"

At least she didn't mince words.

"I showered this morning."

"And yet, you haven't changed out of your pajamas, I see."

They weren't pajamas. Pajamas were sweats, flannels, thermals even, but I knew better than to enter into a debate with her over what was considered night attire and what wasn't.

She shook her head. "What would your grandfather say if he could see you now?"

I was sure he *could* see me now. Just because he'd passed on into some kind of invisible hemisphere, didn't mean he wasn't around in one form or another. At times it was almost like I could feel him with me, standing there by my side, like if I swept a hand through the air, I'd feel him, touch him somehow. That he'd become real again, if only for a moment.

"Why are you here?" I asked. "I thought you were off seeing the world."

"I was … I am. I will be once I get *you* sorted out."

I leaned against the wall, distanced myself from her judgmental finger. "There's nothing to sort out."

"Are you going to tell me what's got you living like a recluse, or do I have to pry it from your bony, underfed body?"

"Somehow I feel like you wouldn't be standing in front of me if you didn't already know, and there's only one person who could have tipped you off."

"If you're hinting at your friend Madison, then yes. She called me. And then I made an effort to reach you. I called five times to be exact."

I shook my head. "I haven't had any calls from you. I would have answered."

"I was out of the country, dear. You wouldn't have identified the number."

Gran was the only person I knew who had yet to embrace the invention of the cell phone. After watching a news program on electromagnetic radiation, she never used her dishwasher again. Or the microwave. A cell phone? Forget about it.

"I'm sorry," I said. "If I knew you were calling, I would have answered. I swear."

"I'm not here for an apology. I'm here to help you out of this … whatever is happening with you lately." She ran a hand through my brown mane. "You've gone and lopped your hair off. When did that happen?"

"Six months ago, I guess."

"I like it. It suits you. You need to get your sassy attitude back to match this sassy pixie cut of yours."

She scrounged around my pantry until she found a single packet of no-name coffee I'd snagged from a prior hotel stay. She brewed it. We sat.

"You were your grandfather's favorite, you know."

I knew. My sister had been my grandmother's favorite. I knew that too.

"He loved all his grandchildren, but you, Sloane…you were different."

"I always thought he was disappointed I didn't join the bureau like he did."

She circled her hand around the coffee mug. "Nonsense. He knew you well enough to know the FBI wouldn't suit you." She tapped the edge of the mug with the tip of her finger. "You've never done well with authority."

I supposed it was the nicest way she could think of to say it. A compliment, even, though it didn't sound like one.

She leaned over, fiddled around the inside of the ostrich Prada handbag next to her, pulled out a navy blue leather book about the size of a pack of cigarettes. I craned my head toward the bag, glanced inside. "What are you packing these days?"

"This little gem."

She dug back inside the bag, handed me what looked like a child's toy. It was far from it. "Nine mil?"

"Beretta, yes. It's small, but it gets the job done."

"You say it like you've used it before."

The telling grin on her face made me uneasy.

"Only at the shooting range, right?" I asked.

She swatted the air, changed the subject. "The sign outside your house says there's a sale pending. Why have you decided to sell this place?"

I hesitated, unsure of how much I wanted to say. Best to keep it simple. "Too many memories."

"Bad ones?"

"Bad enough to make me feel suffocated if I stay."

She took a sip of coffee, screwed up her face like she'd just swallowed a mouthful of pickle juice. I handed her a canister of sugar substitute I kept for occasions such as this one. She dumped about a quarter cup into the mug.

"Running won't solve your problems," she stated.

"I'm not … running. I'm starting over. Clean slate. New life."

She went for taste test number two on the coffee, this time rejecting it all together by scraping the bottom of the mug across the tabletop to get it away from her. "I see. Where will you go?"

I shrugged.

"I figured by the time I sold my place, I'd have it all figured out. I didn't realize it would sell so fast."

She leaned in.

"You mean to tell me my methodical, ever-so-organized granddaughter doesn't have a plan yet? Never thought I'd see the day."

"I can't be here anymore, Gran. People around me … they're *always* in danger. Some have even died."

"So all of this, the hiding, is about your job?"

"It's about a lot of things. I ended a relationship several months ago. I lost a friend on the last case I worked—my ex-boyfriend's brother. Sometimes I wonder—"

"If it's your fault?"

I nodded.

"Do you think your grandfather saved everyone? You can't, Sloane, no matter how noble your efforts. You lost someone on the last case you worked. You also rescued a woman on the brink of death. Your friend didn't die in vain. He died in the line of duty. There's no shame in that."

Saving one life didn't make me feel any better about losing another.

"It's just … I can't unsee all the things I've seen. I don't know how to get my past out of my head. It's hard."

"Who told you it would be easy? Think of the people you *have* saved, the cold cases you've solved on your own. Those cases would be nothing more than a heap of unsolved files rotting in some box were it not for you."

"For every life I've saved, someone else died because I was too late, too slow, too stubborn, too—"

She folded her hand inside mine. "You have a gift, a kind of intuition others don't have, and right now, you're wasting it. You talk about what you do like none of it matters. This isn't like you. I've never seen you back down from a challenge."

"I'm not backing down. I'm—"

"Avoiding. Everyone and everything."

She liberated my hand long enough to plop the navy book down on the table in front of me. It made a slapping sound against the wood.

"What's this?" I asked.

"Your grandfather's journal."

"I didn't know he kept one."

"It's not what you think, a memoir of some kind, a story of his life. It's much different." She stabbed the book's cover with her pointer finger. "This is what he did when his insomnia got the better of him. Your grandfather lost far more lives than you ever will. It troubled him, and yet, he never gave up. He wouldn't want you to either."

"I'm not giving up. I'm taking a break."

"Suppressing yourself like this—you may as well give up. You were destined for greatness, my dear. Even when you were young I could see the fire in you. I'd never seen a child quite so driven. As long as I'm kicking around this Earth, I won't allow you to throw it all away."

I ran the pads of my fingers against the book, caressing the soft, pebbly grain. An odor of seasoned leather and men's aftershave wafted through the air, and for a brief moment I flashed back, saw myself sitting on my grandfather's lap, begging him to tell me a story. Not the kind of story most kids want to hear, the fairy tale with the predictable, happy ending. Grandfather's stories were different. They were real, not make-believe. Intriguing. They created visions in my head that helped shape my own destiny. "What's in the book? His cases?"

"Read it and find out."

I opened it.

She reached over, smacked it closed. "Not now. Later."

"Why later? You just said to read it."

She stood, slid her chair back under the table. "Pack some things."

"What? Why?"

"I'm leaving, and you're coming with me. I've made the necessary arrangements. Maddie will see to the dog while we're away."

Away.

It sounded so … far.

It was.

I spent the next two weeks exfoliating my feet into delicate grains of fine, white sand while I watched the remaining moments of twilight fade into a coral horizon. I filled my lungs with salty, sea air, closed my eyes, and paired my breathing with the rise and fall of each cresting wave. Even if for the briefest of moments, I felt something I hadn't in a long time—complete and utter peace.

I returned to Park City renewed. I signed over my house, put my things in storage, and drove to Wyoming, where I currently festered. It was the first time I'd felt this uneasy since Gran whisked me to the Big Island. Somewhere inside me, I couldn't shake the feeling I had.

Something was wrong.

Something was *very* wrong.

CHAPTER 3

A ray of light danced into the room like a siren begging me to wake. Where was I, and how did I end up here? I glanced around. A knotty pine dresser with resin antler drawer pulls rested a few feet in front of the bed against a log wall.

Cade's house. Right. Now I remember.

I'd embraced sleep sometime before dawn, not for long, an hour, maybe two. I checked the room for a clock. There wasn't one, and I wasn't keen about rising just yet. The mattress I relaxed on was topped with a four-inch memory foam, the perfect temptation to stay right where I was for an undetermined amount of time.

A pungent, meaty aroma emanated through the one-inch slit beneath the bedroom door. At first I pegged it as steak. After inhaling a subsequent whiff, I abandoned the theory, thinking it was some kind of wild game.

Someone tapped on the other side of my door. "You up yet?"

"I'm awake."

Cade entered the room, grinned. "I made breakfast."

"Smells like … meat of some kind?"

"Elk steak."

His grin expanded for a moment then dissipated. "Somethin' wrong?"

I wasn't sure what to say. I'd never eaten elk or any other kind of wild animal before. I explained this, but not wanting to disappoint him, I offered to try it, with a side of eggs to break up the flavor if the taste didn't suit me.

My comment about the eggs on the side got lost in translation, and minutes later, I was greeted at the table by an elk steak omelet. Cade stood beside me, waiting for me to take a bite. I stabbed a piece, stuck it in my mouth, and swallowed. Avoiding the chewing part seemed like an optimal choice under the circumstances. I reached for the apple juice in front of me and half-smiled. "It's … different."

"How'd you know? You didn't leave it in your mouth long enough."

The jig was up.

"I'm not used to this kind of food."

Cade's daughter Shelby sauntered into the room wearing a black-and-white-striped crop top, a black leather skirt, and Chuck Taylors in a shade that made me crave an Orange Julius. The skirt looked like it was the exact length needed to pass the principal's tape measure inspection at school, and not a centimeter more. Her navel showed. Her neon-orange bra straps did too. She'd just started her senior year in high school, and as such, she probably assured herself such a display would garner attention. And she'd be right, except at that moment it was garnering the wrong kind.

Cade crossed his arms in front of him, didn't say a word. He didn't have to. Shelby tilted her chin just enough to notice the infraction he was gawking at. She yanked the shirt lower. It didn't budge. She tried again, got the same result. She patted Cade on the shoulder. "It's okay, Dad. Breathe."

Her amateur charm had no effect.

"You'll change your shirt," he said.

"Dad, I can't—"

"Now."

She snatched a piece of chopped elk off a plate, popped it into her mouth, and winked at me. "Don't worry, you'll get used to the flavor eventually."

I wasn't thrilled. I popped another piece of scrambled elk into my mouth anyway. This time, I even chewed.

"Well?" Cade asked.

It was coarse, tenderer than I imagined, and while it wasn't my favorite meat, it wasn't the worst I'd tasted either. "Not bad."

Shelby reentered the room, a messenger bag slung over her shoulder. Shirt number two was only a couple inches longer than the first one, but it looked like she'd get away with it.

"I'm off," she said. "School starts in ten. You two behave yourselves now."

She picked a piece of bread out of the toaster, slapped on a dollop of cherry jam, and bit down, swiping a finger across her face to catch the red sauce before it leaked onto her chin.

"Aren't you going to wear a sweater or something?" I asked. "Looks like it's cold out today."

She giggled. "You're funny."

I didn't perceive why. When I was young, unlike the other girls in school, those willing to freeze their asses off in order to flaunt their slim, trim physiques, I'd always preferred a warmer, more practical approach. Of course, it may have had something to do with my grandfather drilling into my brain that no man ever bought a cow when free milk was being offered. Not that I'd ever thought of myself as a cow, or a woman available to the highest bidder.

"Wear a sweater," Cade called after Shelby.

"Fine, Dad." she yelled back.

She pivoted and left the room.

Once she was out of sight, a generous portion of laughter I'd been concealing poured out.

"What's so funny?" Cade asked.

"You know she's just going to change back into the first shirt she was wearing once she gets to school, right?"

Confusion coated his face. "Whadd'ya mean? She changed like I asked."

"Go into her room. See if you can find the first shirt she had on." I tugged a bill from my back pocket, snapped it in front of me. "Ten bucks says you can't."

"And what do I get if *I* win?"

I winked. "You won't."

"You're not helpin'."

"Of course I am. I'm offering you the truth."

Determined to prove me wrong, he went to her room. A fair amount of jostling ensued, followed by a few verbal expletives, followed by him exiting the room sans the shirt. Red-faced and out of breath, he said, "How'd you know?"

"I was her age once. It may have been a long time ago, but still."

He whipped around, started down the hall.

"Where you headed?" I asked.

"To improve her wardrobe."

Cade disappeared. In his absence, I scraped the omelet down the garbage disposal. He returned with an armful of what appeared to be his T-shirts. "Let's see how she feels when this is all she has to wear for the next two—"

Cade's cell phone buzzed, temporarily interrupting him from fulfilling his quest. He bent his head toward the kitchen counter where it sat. "Would you?"

I never liked answering other people's phones. I picked it up anyway. "Cade McCoy's phone."

"Who's this?"

The voice was tough, deep, familiar.

"This is Sloane. And you are?"

A long pause followed. "Why you answerin' Cade's phone, if you don't mind me askin'?"

"I do mind. Would you like to leave a message or call back?"

"Neither. I'll speak with Cade. Now."

"He's occupied."

"As fun as this must be for you, I don't have the time, Miss Monroe."

"Neither do I, Chief Rollins."

I pushed the speaker button.

"I need to speak with Cade right away."

The chief's grave tone of voice prompted Cade to toss the shirts to the side. I took the phone off speaker and handed it to him.

"I'm here," Cade said. "What's happened?"

Although both sides of the conversation weren't audible, Cade's playful demeanor deteriorated. He slumped over the counter, weakened, clutching the granite surface as if trying to sustain his weight.

"When did this happen?" Cade uttered into the phone. "And Jack, you're with him now? What has he said? How is he?"

More muffled words were spoken on the opposite end.

"What about the baby?" Cade asked. "Who has Finn?"

The chief replied once more, and Cade said, "I'll be right there."

I watched him slide his cell phone into the front pocket of his jeans. He bent his head over the counter, placed both hands on top of it.

"Cade, what is it? What's wrong?"

"Last night, someone broke into my cousin's house. Jack. He's my mother's sister's kid."

I covered my mouth with a hand. "Is he all right?"

Cade nodded. "He was at work when it happened."

"Does he have a wife? Kids? Was anyone home at the time?"

"Jack's wife, Serena, was found in the nursery. She'd taken a single gunshot wound to the head."

"Is she—"

"Dead? Yeah. Doesn't look like she suffered much, if at all. She died instantly from what they can tell. She's with the coroner now."

"You said nursery."

"They have a new son. Finn."

A sickened feeling filtered through me. "Where is he—the baby?"

Cade's eyes closed. For several seconds he stood, quiet and placid, like he was wrestling impatient emotions from surging to the surface. I entwined a hand inside his, offering a subtle gesture of support. When his eyes reopened, he said, "The baby's gone, Sloane. He's gone."

CHAPTER 4

The sideways glance Chief Rollins gave me when I stepped inside the station with Cade was all bitter and no sweet. He looked wasted and worn, his face unveiling far more wrinkles than the last time I'd seen him. Maybe his job was catching up to him, or maybe it was his age. Either way, there was a sense of borrowed time, like his rugged lifestyle was finally catching up to him.

The chief jerked his head my way. "What's *she* doin' here?"

"Don't see why it matters," Cade replied.

The chief shoved his thick, calloused fingers halfway inside the pockets of his washed-out Wrangler jeans and bent one knee. He leaned back, his python snakeskin boot tapping the wall behind him. "Matters to me. I don't need her pokin' her head where it don't belong, like she did last time she was here."

Cade folded one arm over the other. "And I don't need to remind you that we have Sloane to thank for findin' those missing girls."

While true, it was a fun fact the chief would just as soon forget.

"What we're dealin' with right now, it don't concern her."

The chief had yet to look at me, in the eye anyway. Why not make things even more unpleasant by approaching him myself? "Since I'm standing right in front of you, why not talk to me directly?"

He accepted the challenge. "All right. That doorway you just walked through—use it to show yourself out. I need to speak with Cade. Alone."

Cade muttered something I didn't catch. I didn't need to—his expression said it all.

"It's fine," I said. "His house, his call."

I was an outsider.

I didn't blend in.

I never did.

"I'll leave you two to talk," I said.

Thinking the problem was solved, I turned. "I'll be in the truck."

Cade walked past me, motioned for me to follow.

"Where you goin'?" the chief asked.

"What's it look like?" Cade said. "I'm leavin'."

"Aww, hell, Cade. Not this again."

"Look." Cade glanced back. "Sloane's not hurtin' nothin'. It doesn't have to be this way. If you're gonna be ignorant, I'm leavin'. Your call."

"I'm not here to interfere," I added. "I'm just visiting for the weekend. Besides, I haven't worked a case in months."

The chief raised a brow. "Since when?"

His sudden interest surprised me. "I … needed a break."

"A break, or somethin' else?"

"Meaning?"

"Heard an agent died on your last job," the chief said. "Someone you knew. Heard the feds came down hard on the little PI operation you're runnin'. You throw it in, close up shop?"

"Enough," Cade said. "Cut her some slack."

"Why? She was there when the agent was murdered, wasn't she?"

The chief squinted, his eyes examining mine. He had an exceptional poker face, a skill I'd always lacked. I couldn't tell whether he pitied me or despised me. Maybe it was a combination of both. His mouth opened to dispense even more disparaging comments, but then in an odd moment of silence, he hesitated, which was peculiar for a man who never held back. Whatever he planned on saying, he chose not to say it. Instead, he pointed to a chair positioned outside his office. "Have a seat while I talk to Cade a minute."

The comment stretched the limits of his civility. I accepted it, sitting without another word. Cade followed the chief into his office. The door closed. It didn't matter. There were no curtains or blinds on the chief's window, and his voice carried like a foghorn. He explained Cade's cousin's wife, Serena, had been discovered around seven that morning. Her husband, Jack, had arrived home from work, stopping at the nursery to check on his son before heading to bed.

Jack had entered the baby's room, stunned to find Serena's body sprawled out on the floor, inches away from the crib. Pooled blood stained the rug, forming a ring around Serena's head. Mortified, Jack had initially assumed it was some kind of freak accident. He surmised his wife had slipped on the hardwood floor surrounding the rug. This theory made sense to him, at first. The bottle was several feet away on its side, milk still seeping from the pinhole at the top. He stared at the bottle, then his dead wife, and confusion set in. If her head *had* hit the floor, why was there so much blood?

Legs trembling, Jack had hunched over, looped his hands around the back of his wife's neck. He pulled up. Once her cold, stiff head left the ground, he watched red liquid ooze from a ring-shaped hole in the back of her skull.

Unsure what to do next, Jack had eased his wife back on the ground, his thoughts turning to his infant son. He grappled for the slats on Finn's crib with both hands, easing his weakened knees off the ground into a kneeling position. Battling a siege of tears and legs too rickety to allow him to stand, he stuck his hand in between the wooden bars and reached inside, tugging the baby's blanket toward him. It pulled freely, much easier than he'd anticipated. Once it had passed all the way through the bars and was wadded up between his hands, he knew why. Gazing inside the crib, his worst fear came to light—there was no baby.

Frantic, Jack searched the house, hoping, praying his wife had taken Finn into another room, having only returned to the nursery for a moment to get something she'd forgotten, the baby's bottle, a diaper maybe. There was a realm of possibilities he permitted himself to believe before he accepted the worst. After a hasty, yet thorough search, he had no choice—he came to terms with one gut-wrenching truth: someone had killed his wife, taken their baby.

...

Cade absorbed the chief's summary of the day's events and rattled off several questions: Had the time of death been determined? What had the coroner observed so far? Was there any evidence of foul play? Had the weapon used to kill Serena been recovered? The chief's answers did nothing to soothe him. Not only had no weapon been found, no unidentified prints had been lifted. The point of entry had been established. Even so, they had no leads and no motive—nothing to justify what had been done or why.

The chief attempted to pacify Cade by stating it was still early. Anything could happen.

Cade shook his head, unsatisfied with the chief's simple answers. He requested the scene be processed a second time. He was sure they'd missed something. The chief snapped back with a succinct and final, "No. I will not."

The words "bull" and "shit" were uttered by Cade, followed by a threat I didn't interpret. He said, "If I have to pull rank, Harold, I will."

The chief fired back. "You're not pullin' anything. I'm acting chief on this until the last day of this month. Until we reach the final day, the final hour, the very last second of my command, what I say goes. Understood?"

The door to the chief's office thrust open. Cade glanced in my direction. "We're leaving."

I stood.

"Cade, get back here," the chief demanded. "Sloane, sit back down."

I'd regarded him with courtesy earlier because he was the chief in this town, and as such, no matter what words he spewed my way, he deserved a certain level of respect. When he chose not to reciprocate the same respect to me, the inclination I had to keep the peace between us expired.

"I won't sit down," I responded. "I'm not some lap dog you can order around."

The chief launched a finger at Cade. "You're not workin' this case. You hear me?! You're makin' it personal. I can't have a detective on this who can't keep his head on straight. This is a high-priority case. I won't risk it."

"What are you sayin'?"

"You're out."

Cade kept walking. "Do what you gotta do, Harold. I'll do the same."

Calling Chief Rollins by his first name was a dig on Cade's part, despite the fact he'd known him since he was a child.

Once we were seated inside Cade's truck again, I spoke up. "What happened in there?"

"I think they're missin' somethin'. They have to be. They're about finished searchin' Jack's house, and it isn't even noon yet. I told him to keep the team there, have them go over the place one more time. He took it to mean I'm too emotionally involved to be on the case because Jack's family."

"Your cousin's wife is dead. Their baby missing. Of course you're involved. I grasp why he thinks it would be best for you to take a step back, I just don't agree. If you ask me, he's losing his greatest asset by expecting you to sit on the sidelines. Emotional attachment is what bonds me to a case. It's how I work a case. How I figure things out. Take every emotion you're feeling right now and use it to your advantage. Let it fuel you to find Serena's killer, rescue her baby."

For a pep talk, it wasn't bad.

"You heard what Harold said. I'm off the case. I'm out."

"He's upset," I said. "Let him calm down, recognize how much he needs you."

"I know him better than most. There's one thing he doesn't do—regurgitate his words once he's said 'em."

"Is his permission really necessary?"

He paused, thought about what I just said. "Are you suggestin' I go rogue?"

"I'm suggesting you poke around, conduct your own investigation. Quietly. Away from the chief's radar."

"Ten seconds."

Ten seconds?

"What?"

"I need ten seconds."

Cade placed both hands on the steering wheel, kneading the hardened leather up and down like he was revving an engine. He stared straight ahead, breathed in and out a few times, put a sufficient amount of thought into our conversation. Then he looked at me and grinned. It wasn't the kind of flirtatious, teasing look I'd grown used to, but under the circumstances, even a hint of a smile was better than nothing.

"You're right," he said. "I'm not backin' off. I don't care what he says. He has his team—I have something even better."

"A lead?"

He shook his head, cast a finger my direction. "You."

CHAPTER 5

"Cade, I—"

"Haven't taken anything on in a while," he said. "I know."

He turned in his seat, faced me, grazed my leg with his hand. "Even if I hadn't been kicked off the case, there's no one I'd rather have by my side on this than you. We work great together. You know we do."

"I can't just—"

"Yes, you can."

I was beginning to think finishing a simple sentence was out of the question. His request compelled me to explain why taking on a case, any case, wasn't something I was sure I was up to yet. "These last several months, I've had the chance to envision my life, my past, my present, everything leading up to this moment, the woman I am today."

"And?"

"I became a PI because of an innate desire I have to solve things. I wanted to make a difference, wanted to help people."

"You have."

"The cases I take on are like riddles I contend with until they're solved. They monopolize my life, become my addiction. They're tempting, enticing, a weakness. My weakness."

He dipped his head, half-closed his eyes. "What are you tryin' to say?"

"I'm thinking about getting out of the business."

Saying the words aloud made me feel like a traitor, like I'd branded the center of my forehead with a "Q" for "quitter," abandoning those that would seek me out in the future, request my help.

"Huh."

I didn't know what response I expected, but "huh" wasn't it. Cade revved the steering wheel again for another ten seconds. "There will always be losses along the way. Lives lost, lives saved, lives destroyed, lives rebuilt. With great losses come great wins. Don't let your failures define you, or they'll haunt you until you're consumed with grief from events you never had the ability to control in the first place."

Too late.

I mulled over his words, recognizing it was the loss of control that drove me inside in the first place. Funny thing, control—the power to manage a circumstance, an environment. OCD at its finest. Not as funny when the management is lost.

"Sloane, listen to me. I need you. When Shawn Hurtwick took my daughter, you convinced him to let her go. No one could have done what you—"

My turn to interrupt.

"I'll do it. I'll help you."

Whether it was the right decision or the wrong one, I wasn't sure. I was only certain of one thing—ever since we'd met, he'd been there for me, by my side, helping me whenever I asked. I couldn't refuse him. Not now. Not when he needed me.

"You will?"

"If you're going to do this on your own—"

"Not on my own," he corrected. "Together."

"All right, *together* … we need to keep this quiet for now. I don't want to get you in any trouble."

"Since when has anything you've done *not* led to trouble?" he teased. "Won't matter much longer, anyway."

"Why not? Are you going to tell me your news?"

"You heard me—in there?"

I nodded. "What did you mean in the chief's office? You mentioned you could pull rank. What happens at the end of the month?"

"I know I asked you here to celebrate sellin' your house. In truth, I was hopin' we'd celebrate somethin' else too. I'm takin' over Harold's job."

"Chief Rollins is retiring?"

"Yep. Got the call from the town administrator a few days ago sayin' the job's mine if I want it. I planned on surprisin' you with the news tonight. Then I got the call this mornin', heard what happened, and … I guess I don't feel much like celebratin' anymore."

I didn't blame him. "I have an idea."

"Shoot."

"We find Finn, give your cousin and his family some peace of mind, and when you feel up to it, I'll throw the party."

He stuck his hand out, formalizing the arrangement. "Darlin', you've got yourself a deal."

CHAPTER 6

Loss is a powerful thing, an axe slowly chipping away at a person's soul. After each death, each devastation, another fragment breaks off, slips through the cracks, gone forever. There's no repairing the damage, no going back, no returning to life as it was before. Death doesn't work that way.

Death doesn't give—it takes. One day you're kissing your loved one goodbye, the next day they're gone forever, ripped from your arms, often without warning. The survivors, those who rise above the unexpected loss, spend the rest of their lives in repair mode, searching for the chipped pieces they've lost, thinking if they find them, they can somehow be reattached.

They can't.

They never will.

Not in this lifetime.

And maybe not even in the next.

Even when the anguish fades away, the memories linger, the smallest reminder becoming a trigger to a time long past.

I witnessed loss in people's faces every day. The prolonged glance out the car window on a long drive, the intense longing of someone staring at a bent, faded picture, the touch of a precious relic, passed down, left behind.

Jack Westwood was experiencing this very kind of grief right now, except for him, it was just beginning. He slouched back on a brown leather sofa, his face in a dizzy fog, eyes staring out his living room window at a tree in his front yard. At least, he appeared to be staring. I doubted he was focused on any one thing. His eyes, puffy and damp, made him appear allergic to every kind of pollen known to man. Given his relation to Cade, I expected he'd look like a rough and tough cowboy, a vigorous man full of pride. He didn't. He didn't look like anyone really, except a tortured man mourning the abrupt loss of his wife.

When I'd arrived at Jack's house with Cade, we were polite, respectful, ringing the doorbell twice before turning the knob and letting ourselves inside. Jack hadn't looked up when we entered the room, hadn't seemed the least bit interested in who was there or why.

In his hands, he clutched a cardboard box so tight I could see white protruding from his knuckles.

"I'm sorry, Jack," Cade said.

Jack remained silent, stared outside into the abyss, unmoved by Cade's expressed compassion. We waited, tuned in to the ticking of an oval-shaped clock resting on the fireplace mantle. One minute passed, then two. After the third came and went, Cade started fidgeting. "We need to talk, when you're ready. If this isn't a good time, we'll come back later."

A good time.

Good times no longer existed for Jack.

Jack separated the lid from the box, let it fall to the side. He reached inside, ran a mass of blue fabric between his fingers, started rambling. "This coat came for Rena today."

Rena. Must have been his nickname for his wife.

"I ordered it for her birthday," Jack continued. "We were shopping a couple weeks ago. She saw it. Said she liked it, but they didn't have it in her size. I ordered it for her as a surprise. She would have been forty next week. I was going to throw her a party. And now I … she won't ever … I don't know how I can … I don't know what I'm supposed to do now, Cade."

"I'll find whoever did this, Jack," Cade said. "I promise."

For as tough as Cade was, his words were choppy, difficult to get out.

"Why? Why would someone take her from me? Why take our baby?"

"I don't have the answers you need right now," Cade replied. "I swear to you, you *will* have them."

Salty tears dripped like a leaky faucet, trailing down Jack's face, and I found myself brushing one of my own to the side. Sympathizing with a deceased person's spouse was part of the job, but not a part I relished. I suppose I could have been more diplomatic, unaffected. Professional. My heart allowed for many things. Pretending I was inhuman wasn't one of them.

The coat slithered through Jack's hands, puddled around his feet. His fingers hung in the air, pressed together like he hadn't noticed the coat had plummeted from his grasp. It concerned me. I looked around, lifted an empty glass off of an old desk, took a whiff.

Whiskey.

I canvassed the room for the bottle and found one tipped over on the floor behind the sofa. The lid wasn't screwed on all the way, but the carpet was dry. The bottle was half empty. I picked it up, showed it to Cade.

"Jack," Cade asked, "how much whiskey have you had today?"

"Don't know. Two ... three?"

"Two or three what?"

"Glasses."

"Straight?"

Jack shrugged.

Cade shifted his gaze to me. "He doesn't drink. Never has."

I swirled the liquid around inside the bottle. "Today he does."

A red truck pulled up, parked. It was vintage. Restored. A Chevy maybe or a Dodge with a rounded hood. Seconds later the front door opened and closed.

"Jack, you around?"

The voice was a woman's.

"In here," Cade replied.

"Cade, is that you?"

A long-haired brunette walked into the room, her curls bouncing up and down with each forward movement. She was dressed in a tight-fitting, plaid flannel shirt, corduroy pants, and leather, square-toed boots with red bull heads stitched on the sides. She walked over to the couch and plopped down, kissing Jack on the cheek, running a hand through his short, blond hair. She gestured toward me. "Who's this?"

"Sloane," Cade answered.

She bobbed her head up and down like we were already acquainted. "Park City Sloane?"

I looked at Cade. He dodged the question. Unfortunately for him, the girl kept on talking. "Cade talks about you all of the—"

Cade scrutinized the woman like she was a ticking time bomb waiting to go off. "Grace, let's have this conversation in the other room."

Once we were in the kitchen, out of earshot, I seized the moment. "So ... what has Cade said about me, exactly?"

Grace slid a wooden chair out from under a table, sat down, gestured for me to do the same. She pretended not to notice the intense look Cade gave her from across the room. "Ahh ... you know what? I'd better not say anything else. Cade might never forgive me."

"I don't mean to seem rude," I said, "but who are you?"

"Jack's sister."

"Which makes you—"

"Cade's cousin." She frowned. "Serena was one of my closest friends."

Cade weaved one boot over the other, leaned against the kitchen counter. "Now that the formalities are out of the way, let's change topics. Jack's not talkin'. Maybe it's because he's liquored up at present, but I can't help him if I don't have a place to start, and he's it."

Grace rapped the tips of her fingers on the edge of the table. "Can you blame him? He's in shock."

"'Course I don't blame him. If this was happening to one of us, we'd all react the same way."

"The fact is, he's not up to the kind of conversation you're after," Grace said. "Not right now. Why don't you tell me what you know so far? Maybe I can help."

"Chief Rollins said Jack was at work last night. Came home this morning, found Serena dead, Finn gone. Whoever did this was clean, wore gloves, didn't leave any prints behind, not even a partial."

"No sign of forced entry?" Grace asked.

"I was told he entered through a window in the basement."

"How do you know?"

"The chief said the metal on the latch was broken off. When police arrived this morning, they noticed the window wasn't shut all the way. The ledge was dusty. One part was smudged like someone had gripped it for balance while they broke into the house."

"Anything else?"

"The front door was locked and bolted. The back door was open."

Grace perked up. "That's how he escaped. Must have walked right out the back door."

"You sure?"

"Positive," Grace said. "I was here last night. I saw her. We talked. When I left, she seemed fine."

Cade walked to the back door. Opened it. Inspected the knob, the lock, the door jamb. "If he exited this way, he showed himself out. This door only locks from the inside, unless you have a key. I'm guessin' he didn't. What time were you here?"

"Around nine fifteen, nine thirty. Serena called me. She was out of formula and didn't want to wake the baby and take him out so late at night. I offered to run to the store. When I got here, I pulled around back. She unlocked the door, let me in. We talked."

"For how long?"

"Half hour, maybe."

"Jack told police he spoke to her on the phone around nine, which would have been right before you arrived. You were the last one to talk to her, the last one to see her alive."

"She was in good spirits when I was here. Everything was fine. I left the same way I came in, and I'm sure she locked the door after me."

"How sure?"

"I heard it click. Besides, she never left things unlocked. Not after Jack started working nights."

Jack stumbled into the room. "Why are you all in here talking about me?"

Cade placed his hand on Jack's arm. Jack lurched back.

"I don't want you here," Jack slurred. "Any of you. I want to be alone."

"Jack," Cade said, "take a minute. Catch your breath. We're only tryin' to help."

"I want you to go, Cade. All of you. Just go."

"It's going to be—"

Through gritted teeth, Jack said, "No, it's not. Rena is dead. My son is gone. Get … out!"

Jack lunged at Cade, attempting to force him out of the way. He missed by a good six inches, plowing head-first into the side of the fridge.

Cade stepped back and spread his hands, holding them out in front of him. "All right, Jack. I hear you. We're leaving."

The three of us stepped outside. I heard the lock click into place, just like Grace heard earlier. Frustrated and unsure of the best way to help her brother, Grace took out her phone, dialed.

"Who are you calling?" I asked.

"Our mother. He needs her. She was on her way out of town this morning. Had a vacation planned with one of her friends. She turned around as soon as she heard the news. Hopefully she's close. You two can go. I'll stay until she gets here."

"My gut says Finn was taken intentionally," Cade said, "which means Serena may have been killed because she got in the way."

"We need to figure out the motive behind the kidnapping," I added.

Grace piped up. "I can think of one person with a reason."

Cade's eyes widened. "Who?"

"The birth mother."

"What birth mother?" I asked.

"Finn was adopted," Cade said. "Serena couldn't have children."

"What does the birth mother have to do with this?" I asked.

"Everything," Grace said. "She never wanted to give up the baby."

CHAPTER 7

Grace's declaration shocked me. "What? Wait a minute. How do you know the birth mother wanted to keep the baby?"

"Serena told me," Grace answered.

"Did Jack know?"

"About the girl's reservations? Kinda."

Kinda?

I probed for more.

"Whatever Serena told you, we need to know everything. All of it. Don't leave anything out."

Grace looked at Cade like she sought his approval before disclosing the rest.

"Sloane's right," he said. "We need to know what you know. You need to make Chief Rollins aware of it too."

I imagined he wanted to keep the conversation between the three of us. Telling the chief wasn't ideal, but she had information the chief didn't. It was the right thing to do.

"Serena never met the birth mother until the night the baby was born," Grace said.

"What about before Finn was born?" I asked. "Did they talk?"

Grace nodded. "On the phone, several times."

"Is that … allowed?"

"As long as both parties agree to it. The birth mother was trying to choose between Serena and Jack and another couple. She had a few questions before she made her final decision. Serena wasn't sure she wanted to make phone contact at first."

"She did though, right?"

"Yes. She was afraid if she denied the calls, she'd anger the birth mother, and the other couple would be chosen."

"What did they talk about?"

"The girl—"

"Does this girl have a name?" I asked.

"Hannah Kinkade. She wanted to know about Jack and Serena's background, why they wanted a baby, how long they'd been married, whether they planned to adopt more children, that type of thing. Serena wasn't obligated to answer. She wanted to put Hannah's mind at ease."

"You said they never saw each other *before* the baby was born. What about after?"

"Jack and Serena waited outside the delivery room while Hannah gave birth."

The surprises kept coming. "Hannah allowed them to be there? Is that common?"

Grace shrugged. "Serena thought Hannah offered because Hannah wanted to get a better feel for who she was giving her baby to before she signed his life away to someone else."

"I can't even imagine how tough that would be," I said.

"It was one of the hardest things Serena's ever gone through."

Cade scooted onto the seat in his truck, allowed me to do what I did best.

"If Serena had been trying so long for a baby, I would think it would have been one of the best days of her life."

Grace dug divots into the grass using the heel of her boot. "Yeah, Serena thought it would be. "Magical" was the word she used before the birth. Afterward, Serena could see how much of a struggle it was for Hannah to let the baby go. She didn't expect it."

"Did Hannah ever *say* she didn't want to give up the baby?" I asked.

"Hannah didn't, no."

"Then how did Serena know? She assumed it?"

"Hannah's aunt was also there. She mentioned how difficult the decision had been."

"Do you remember the aunt's name?"

"I believe Serena said her name was Renee. She asked if Serena and Jack would consider allowing her niece to have visitation once in a while. When Serena asked why, the aunt said a few days prior to giving birth, Hannah started talking about keeping the baby. The aunt thought if Jack and Serena allowed Hannah to see him once in a while, it would give Hannah the push she needed to sign the paperwork."

In college, one of my classmates had learned she was pregnant after a brief, one-night stand with a man she met at a bowling alley of all places. She didn't know the man's name or where he lived. She didn't even know his phone number. She didn't think she needed it. The guy was supposed to have been a one-night, one-time thing. Then she missed her period. Against her parents' request to raise the child themselves, when the child was born, a girl, she handed her over to an adoption agency, opting for a closed adoption. She never saw her daughter again. Until now, this was the only knowledge I had of the adoption process. Either times had changed or Finn's adoption was a lot more complicated.

"I'm assuming Hannah didn't choose a closed adoption?" I asked.

"She wanted it to be open. Serena and Jack said no. Hannah then asked for semi-open, and they agreed to it."

"I'm not sure I know how to distinguish the different types."

"Semi-open means Serena and Jack agreed to send photos of the baby and letters about how the baby was doing to the adoption agency from time to time. The agency then forwarded the letters to Hannah. This allowed them to share some information while keeping other things about their private lives confidential."

"Seems so strange."

"Not really. It's designed to protect the identity of everyone involved while also allowing for a connection. Some families go way beyond this. It's all about what's comfortable for everyone involved."

"Doesn't it change once the baby is legally adopted by the adoptive family?" I asked.

"In a closed adoption, yes. Semi-open is different. And with open adoption, there's even more involvement between the birth parents and adoptive parents. The lady Serena worked with at the adoption agency told Serena one of her other adoptive families had just attended their birth mother's graduation—and they'd adopted the baby two years before."

"How was it supposed to work for Serena and Jack?"

"Hannah was only supposed to know what they looked like, their first names, what they did for a living, that kind of thing. Basic details. Nothing too private."

"Why do I get the feeling Hannah knew a lot more?" I asked.

"After Finn's birth, Serena was afraid Hannah wouldn't sign the baby over, so she verbally agreed to let Hannah see him once every six months. She hoped after some time passed, Hannah would change her mind, move on with her life. She was so young, just starting out in life. Way too young to focus on raising a baby."

Grace closed her eyes, sighed.

"What is it?" I asked.

"A week after Finn was born, Hannah showed up on Jack and Serena's front porch, violating the agreement they made."

"Wait—I thought you said Hannah didn't know where they lived?"

"According to the adoption agency, she didn't."

"Then how did she know where to find them?" I asked.

"Hannah wouldn't say."

"What *did* she say?"

"She said she made a mistake. She begged for her baby back."

Cade, who appeared to have only been partially attentive to the conversation, gave me a look like "let's go," which I didn't know how to interpret. Grace was giving me the kind of information we needed. Information no one else had.

I held up a finger, turned back toward Grace. "Did Serena call the police after Hannah arrived?"

Grace shook her head. "She felt sorry for her. Hannah could barely speak. She seemed—desperate."

"How did Serena handle it?"

"She said she'd allow Hannah to see Finn if Hannah let her have her aunt's phone number. Serena called. Renee came right over, promised she'd make sure Hannah never bothered them again."

"And?"

"She didn't. At least not from what Serena told me. Serena made it clear that if it happened again, she'd get the police involved. Cade would have heard about it if she did."

Cade stuck his head out of the truck window, his impatience escalating. "Sloane, we need to go."

I thanked Grace and speed-walked my way to Cade's truck. I expected him to start the engine. He didn't. I opened the passenger-side door and turned back. "Grace, can I ask you one more question?"

I didn't bother looking at Cade. Whatever was going on, he wasn't happy.

"Sure, what is it?"

"If Hannah didn't want to go through with the adoption, why did she? You said she was young, but it's obvious she wasn't keen on giving up her baby."

"Serena told me the boyfriend pressured her to give the baby up."

"Who?"

"Hannah's boyfriend. The birth father."

CHAPTER 8

Questions mounted in my mind. Why did Hannah's boyfriend want her to give up the baby if he knew Hannah wanted to keep it? Why hadn't Hannah just ended the relationship? And the biggest question of all—why was Hannah's aunt the only one in the delivery room? Why weren't Hannah's parents there when she gave birth?

My focus changed. I thought about Grace, whom I considered to be a stoic rock in a world of emotional pebbles. If Serena's death stirred her emotions, she didn't show it.

I turned to Cade. "For someone who just lost her close friend and sister-in-law, Grace doesn't seem affected by what's going on."

"Sloane …"

"She just seems so pleasant and calm considering—"

"Sloane," Cade said, again. "Grab somethin' and hang on."

"What? Why?"

A toothpick dangled from his mouth. He rolled it around, using it as a pointer. "See the van parked at the end of the street?"

I squinted, impressed with his hawk-like vision.

"They've been sittin' there since we walked outside," he continued. "Idling."

"You didn't have to wait for me. You could have checked them out."

"I wanted to see what they'd do first. I think they've been waitin',"

"For what?"

"Us to leave."

"Why?"

"We're about to find out."

Cade ignited the engine, hammered down on the gas pedal. The inhabitants of the van entered a state of unprepared shock. The van jolted back, then throttled forward, tires squealing along the damp pavement. With both pairs of eyes fixed on Cade's fast-approaching vehicle, they missed something important—a third vehicle turning down the road.

The van collided with a bronze-colored Cadillac, side-swiping the sedan on the driver's side. Metal crunched and glass shattered, spraying shards of debris through the open air like piñata bursting at the seams. Cade thrust the truck into park and leapt out, sprinting to the sedan. The airbag inside the car had deployed moments earlier, blocking me from seeing the driver.

I had a clear view of the van. Both passengers appeared to be involved in an argument of some kind. I exited the truck, acutely aware of the high-pitch scream echoing behind me. I turned, watched Grace race up the street toward us. I looked at her then at Cade. Clarity came, and suddenly I was aware of who the mysterious person was sitting behind the wheel of the Cadillac.

Grace and Jack's mother.

CHAPTER 9

"Mom!" Grace was alarmed but incredibly cool-headed at the same time.

"She's all right," Cade shouted.

He had the door of the Cadillac open and was hunched over his aunt's body, feeling around, making sure nothing was broken before he elevated her from the seat.

"I'm fine, Cade," the woman shouted. "Stop fussing!"

Cade ignored her request and waved me over. "Make sure those two idiots don't go anywhere."

Based on his tone of voice, I assumed he'd recognized the van's passengers.

I approached the vehicle. The exchange between the van's occupants had escalated to fever pitch. They didn't notice me. Not even when I tapped on the glass with my fingernail. A far more attention-grabbing approach was in order. I jerked the drivers-side door open. "Out!"

Shocked into silence, they reeled their heads toward me. The female in the driver's seat had sustained a few gashes to her head, a scrape or two on one of her arms, nothing major. The man beside her was fine, due in part to the fact his seatbelt was buckled. Hers wasn't.

"Who are *you?*" the man asked.

"Yeah," the woman added. "I don't recall seeing you around here before."

"Who I am isn't important," I replied. "I asked you to exit your vehicle, and when I ask someone to do something, I only ask once."

The man thumbed in my direction. "I like her. She's funny."

"Get out or I'll drag you out. Your choice."

The man's eyes flashed with excitement. "You must be new."

The woman cupped a hand over her mouth, whispered loud enough for me to hear. "I bet she's McCoy's replacement once he snags Rollins' job."

I opened the driver's side door.

"Okay, okay," the woman leveled her hands in front of her. "We got it—we're getting out."

"Yeah," the man laughed, palms raised, "don't shoot."

It took every ounce of what little restraint I'd been blessed with for me not to brandish the pistol I'd stashed in my jacket pocket earlier that morning. Anything to sequester their incessant giggling.

I peeked into the back of the van. Saw camera equipment. Lots of it. And based on the lilac-colored blazer the forty-something-year-old woman wore and her sprayed-to-immovable-perfection blond locks, I deduced the only threat they posed was the exposure kind.

"You hit another car, possibly injuring the other person in the process," I said, "or worse. Can you two at least stop acting like a couple of jackasses and pretend like you care?"

The man swished a hand through the air. "Bonnie's fine. It'll take a lot more than a wee fender bender to take her out, I assure you." He stretched out his hand. "Name's Joe Rigby, and this is Shonda Pierce."

"I assume you're with a news channel?"

They nodded in unison.

"Why did you two take off when you saw us coming?" I asked.

Shonda spoke first. "We're not *really* supposed to be here. Well, not yet. That's what we were arguing about. When Joe saw Detective McCoy walking out of

Jack Westwood's house, he wanted to leave. I wanted to stay, and since I was driving—"

"You haven't answered my question. Why were you staking out the house in the first place? The family is grieving. They're not accepting interviews. You have no right to be here."

Joe and Shonda exchanged glances. "We were just waiting until we received confirmation."

"On what? A husband is mourning his wife, a father is missing his child. If you think you're going anywhere near Jack, now or in the near future, think again."

Shonda patted down her stiff hair. It barely moved. "We're not here about what happened last night. We're here about what happened today."

"Nothing *happened* today."

Shonda raised a brow. She turned to Joe who tugged at his jawline with his fingers.

"You mean to say you don't know?" Joe asked.

"Don't know what?"

Shonda snapped her mouth shut and zigzagged her arms, stared at a patchy piece of grass shooting out of a crack in the pavement.

I turned to Joe, hoping they weren't both going to clam up. "Well, looks like it's up to you to tell me what's really going on here."

"There was … umm … what we heard anyway … I need you to realize none of this has been confirmed yet, which is why we didn't approach Jack in person …"

Good hell.

"Spit it out, Joe," I said.

"There was a baby found today."

It was like the entire neighborhood held its breath. There was no sound. No movement. Nothing but deathlike noiselessness.

In an instant Cade's fists encased the collar of Joe's jacket. "Where was the baby found? Where?!"

"Five hours from here in Ogden, Utah."

"Whatever it is you're not tellin' us, you've got about five seconds to—"

Joe writhed around, freed himself from Cade's grip. "Whoa … now hold on, detective. All we know is the baby they found was a boy. An infant. Not sure how old. Not even sure if the kid's related to this case or not. We've been waiting to find out whether or not he's Jack's boy."

"The baby," Cade asked. "What do you know about him?"

"Like I said before, not much."

"Is he alive? Dead?"

Joe hesitated, reluctant to answer. "From what we've been told, he's dead."

CHAPTER 10

In the early morning hours, a baby had been found zipped inside a nylon duffel bag that had been discarded on the shoulder of the I-15 freeway between Logan and Bountiful, Utah. Although it was too soon to tell, based on the acute fractures the child suffered ante mortem, the first medical team to reach the scene suspected foul play, an obvious presumption. The ME asserted the baby had most likely been heaved from a vehicle, *while* the vehicle was still in motion. Whether the boy had died before or after his tragic exit from the vehicle was still unknown.

I needed answers.

Now.

And I knew who could give them to me.

I dialed Maddie's number.

"How's your weekend going?" Maddie asked.

"Nothing like I thought. How's Boo?"

"Fine. He's missing you though."

"I may need you to keep him a little longer. Is that okay?"

"Of course." The familiar sound of gum cracked in the distance. She'd never been the quietest chewer. "Does your decision to stay longer have anything to do with you finally admitting your feelings for Cade?"

She surmised too much.

"I ... umm ... took a case."

The tone of her voice spiked, going up several octaves. "Really? That's great! I knew you wouldn't be able to give it up."

I stayed quiet.

"Hey, you there?"

"Yeah."

"What's wrong?" she asked.

"I need a favor."

"Sure, name it."

As one of the best MEs in the state of Utah, Maddie frequently came in handy. She'd broken the rules for me on several occasions, trusting me with information I otherwise wouldn't have access to, information that had allowed me to solve some of my hardest cases. We'd worked well together over the years, even though there'd been a handful of times when her over-exuberant, high-octane personality got us into trouble. Even when it did, we'd always made a good team.

"Have you heard about the baby found inside the duffel bag?"

"Yeah, everyone in my circle has," she said. "It's all over the news. Wait—the baby isn't your case, right?"

"I'm not sure yet. Who's the coroner?"

"Hardy. Why?"

"How well do you know him?"

"Her," she said. "Why?"

"What do you know so far?"

"If I tell you, are you going to stop asking questions and tell me why you're asking?"

"Yes."

"They found the infant around five this morning. The officer who spotted the bag thought it was someone's luggage or school bag, at first. Imagine his surprise when he looked inside. Twisted. I can't believe it myself."

"How bad did the baby look?"

"Bad enough," she said. "From what I heard, there's some visible bruising, scrape marks on the baby's hands and face. Haven't seen any pictures though, so the abrasions could have been caused by the freeway. They're checking traffic cameras, trying to find out how he ended up on the road, establishing a time frame of how long he was out there before anyone caught sight of him. Now … why are you so interested? I assume you're working another missing child case?"

I filled her in on the day's events, told her everything I knew.

"Tell Cade I'm sorry," she said when I finished. "Are they close—Cade and his cousin?"

"I'm not sure. He hasn't said. Seems like he had a good relationship with his entire family though."

"How can I help?"

"I need a photo of the baby's face. Can you get it?"

"Yeah, shouldn't be a problem. I'll make a phone call, see what I can do. If I get any grief, I'll drive over, look at the little one myself."

"I appreciate it, Maddie. Right now a photo is the fastest way for me to determine if we're talking about the same baby."

"For Cade's family's sake and for yours, I hope not."

CHAPTER 11

In a bizarre moment of deja vu, I found myself back where we started an hour before, on Jack's front lawn. This time Cade, Bonnie, and Grace were huddled together in the group, swapping information with each other. The reckless reporter and her sidekick were gone. After filling out an accident report, they departed under the watchful eye of us all, knowing full well what would happen if they returned again.

Bonnie had a husky look to her, and the demeanor of a woman who plucked the feathers off her own chickens before tossing them into the cooking pot. She had the kind of face that had never been on the receiving end of anti-wrinkle cream, and yet, I could tell by looking at her that she'd lived a full life, probably a fuller one than most people did.

A tow truck had been called for Bonnie's car. So far, it hadn't arrived. She waited, hands positioned on her hips, pointer finger tapping the leather strap on the belt tied around her waist. "I believe I've had all the excitement I can handle today. Besides, it's a bit damp out here for my liking. Why don't we all go inside?"

"He locked us out," Grace said.

"So you said on the phone earlier," Bonnie replied. "What I can't make sense of is why you all let him get away with it."

"We were just trying to be respectful, Mom. He's a mess."

"Exactly. That's why whether he likes it or not, he's letting us in."

Bonnie marched her way to the front door, banged on the outside with her fist. "Jack, it's your mother. Open up." Her patience expired a full twenty seconds later when she added, "Fine! You don't want to come to the door, I *will* get my tire iron, I *will* put it through one of these fancy front windows of yours, and I *will* come in. Door or window, Son? Choice is yours."

Another thirty seconds and her fear tactic hadn't yielded any positive results. She muttered something sarcastic under her breath while pressing a round, blue button on her key chain. The trunk of her car popped open. She seemed satisfied. "Well, whadd'ya know? Trunk latch still works."

"Aunt Bonnie," Cade said, "now hold on just a—"

She ignored him, outstretched an arm in his direction like she was on stage with the Supremes. "Watch and learn, Cade. Watch and learn."

I think I'd just met my new favorite person.

Bonnie removed the tire iron from the trunk as promised and hoisted it into the air, so if Jack *was* watching, he'd see her intent was real. I glanced at the house. A hand brushed aside a sheer curtain draped in front of the interior window. He *had* seen. He *was* watching. I wondered if this meant he would open the door, and what would happen if he didn't. Had Bonnie really meant what she said?

Cade looked like he believed she did. And yet, he did nothing to stop her. I imagine it was because she was Jack's mother, and as such, he trusted she knew the best way to get through to her son, or anyone, for that matter.

Halfway back to the porch, tire iron in hand, the front door swung open. Jack stood cautiously behind it. He poked his head out, glanced at each of us, turned, and skulked down the hall, defeated.

Bonnie walked in, the first words from her mouth being, "Hand over the liquor, Son."

He disappeared for a short time and returned holding the bottle I'd discovered earlier and a brown paper sack containing two more of the same.

"Is this all of it?" Bonnie asked.

"Yep," he said.

"No lies?"

"No lies."

Bonnie turned on the tap, removed the lids from the bottles, and dumped about a hundred dollars' worth of whiskey down the drain like it was nothing more than a forty-four-ounce soda from the gas station. She filled a glass with water and planted it on the table in front of him. "Drink this."

"I don't feel like—"

"Son, I'm not askin'. Now do it."

Once Jack was sorted out, Bonnie set her sights on me. "I don't think we've been introduced yet, hun."

I started to stand. She flailed her arms in front of her. "Sit, sit. You can skip the formalities. I'm about as informal as they come."

"Sloane Monroe."

Grace grinned at Bonnie who half-closed one eye, assessing me in a whole new light. "Cade's Sloane?"

Cade's Sloane?

The insinuations were getting harder for me to withstand.

"You all right?" Bonnie asked, eyes riveted on me. "Didn't mean to make you uncomfortable. It's just …

well … nice to finally see the woman he's always going on about."

Cade tensed, although I could tell a part of him found it amusing. "We're friends, Bonnie. Nothin' more."

"Nothing more—yet," Bonnie added, stifling a laugh.

I sensed Bonnie didn't hesitate to verbalize any thought or inclination once it entered her mind. Unnerved, I shifted my focus to Jack, watching him sip the water he'd been given like it tasted stale. With his wrist lengthened in front of him, I noticed a black, one-inch initial "R" tattoo. Earlier he'd called his late wife Rena. Must have been what the tattoo stood for. I gawked a few seconds too long, and he caught me staring. He rubbed over the ink with his other hand, shielding it from view.

"I'm … sorry," he said, "for earlier. I'm not usually … I mean to say, I don't act this way."

"You can act whatever way you need to," I said. "Throw a fit, scream, put your fist through a wall if you want. You have every right."

"Want to know what I really want? Sleep. No dreams, just sleep, so I can forget any of this ever happened."

"You might think it's better to be alone. I've been where you are right now. I've gone through what you're going through. Not with a spouse, with my sister. I've pushed people away and locked myself inside, thinking one day I'd wake up and it would all be better. Better is embracing the love all around you. What I'm trying to say is—your family is here to support you. Let them."

Bonnie smiled at Cade. "This one's a keeper."

My phone vibrated in my pocket.

"Where's the restroom?" I asked.

Three individual fingers pointed the way. Once inside, I picked the phone out of my back pocket, instantly aware of the photo attachment I'd received from Maddie. Before opening it, I peered out the bathroom door. Seeing no one, I slid into the master bedroom. On the dresser was a photo of Finn. Next to him on each side were his parents, smiling for the camera, smiling like they didn't have a care in the world. A few weeks ago, they didn't.

I pressed on the attachment link from Maddie, inhaled a lungful of air, braced myself for whatever might appear on the screen in front of me. The baby's face, thin and pale, wasn't what I expected. His tiny, fragile eyes were closed. He looked like he was sleeping. He looked like he was at peace. The scratches he had were minimal. Still, I wanted to run a finger along his sweet face, smoothing even the smallest blemish away.

Staring at the photo in the frame and then back at my digital screen, I was about seventy-five-percent sure my assumption about whether the boy was Finn or not was accurate. Seventy-five wasn't good enough. I needed all one hundred before I had the confidence to make an announcement.

"It's sad, you know." Bonnie entered the room, arms folded. "For years they had one dream, one desire—to find a way to have a child of their own. They finally achieve it, and now this. Doesn't seem fair, does it?

"No, it doesn't."

"In my years I've learned life is just as sour as it is sweet."

I turned the screen of my phone away from her. "Are you married?"

"Widowed. A couple of years gone now."

"I'm sorry."

"Don't be. Hal was my everything. We had a wonderful life together. He lived to see our children grow up, marry. He fulfilled every dream he had. His life was cut short, it's true, but he went out on top, bucket list complete, just like I always knew he would."

There was a moment of awkward silence between us while I pondered what I was about to say, and whether she was the right person to say it to.

"You going to show me what you've got there …
whatever you were staring at with such intensity when I
entered the room?"

"I was trying to decide whether I should or not," I
said.

There was nothing as refreshing as a dose of
honesty from time to time.

"Is it what I think it is?"

"A photo of the baby they found in Utah? Yes. I
need someone to verify if the boy in the photo is Finn or
not. If you're uncomfortable, I understand. I can ask
someone else."

"You've had the privilege of spending the last
couple hours with me. What do you think?"

"I think you're one of the strongest women I've
ever met."

Second only to my grandmother, and Maddie.

My high regard pleased Bonnie.

"I've been blessed to live the kind of raw, rugged
lifestyle most girls are shielded from," she said. "There's
little I can't handle, whether it be in this life or the next,
though far off it may well be."

I thought of Grace and the presumptuous opinion
I'd formed of her earlier. She couldn't help the way she
was. Listening to Bonnie, I gained a better perception of
how Grace was brought up, why she seemed indifferent

to Serena's murder. Who was I to determine how she was truly feeling? If anyone was guilty at masking their true feelings, their true self, it wasn't them. It was me.

The screen on my phone had timed out, dimmed to black. I pressed a button, watched it spark to life again.

Bonnie leaned over, viewed the photo. "That's not Finn."

"Are you sure? Are you absolutely positive?"

"Hun, I've visited this house every single day since my grandbaby graced this earth with his presence. And I'm telling you … that's not our boy."

CHAPTER 12

The sting of disbelief pricked my skin like needles on a hot day. Even if by the tiniest grain of sand, there was hope we'd be able to find him. Hope Finn *was* alive. Statistically, of the percentage of kidnapped children, babies rarely went missing. This truth left me with even more questions.

By the time the police station was notified that Finn was missing, and an AMBER Alert was sent out, the three-hour window, known as the most critical hours to find a child alive, had passed. Even so, I had to ask myself—who could be cruel enough to kill a baby?

Finn's abduction was peculiar, unlike anything I'd investigated before. The adoption factor, coupled with the knowledge Hannah Kinkade regretted giving up her baby, put Hannah at the front of the line on my short list of suspects. With Jack in the most capable of hands and daylight fading fast, Cade and I made our exit.

Serena's recent phone logs produced the number Serena had used to call Hannah's aunt the day of Hannah's unfavorable visit. The aunt's full name was Renee Kinkade. From there, finding an address proved easy. I just hoped we weren't too late.

We drove across town without engaging in much conversation. Cade hummed along to a classic Bonnie Raitt tune on the radio, while I gazed at the Wyoming skyline. It was vibrant and alive, its pastel shades of pink and blue swirling together like billowy layers of cotton candy. Of all the places I'd been in my life, Wyoming sunsets were spectacular, the grandest I'd ever seen.

"I hate to admit it," I said, "but I pegged Grace all wrong."

"Whadd'ya mean?"

"She didn't seem too shaken up over what happened to Serena. At first I took it to mean they weren't as close as she led on. Now I know I was mistaken."

"Grace is a bottler."

"A what?"

"She isn't big on feelings. She always keeps her emotions under control. Been like that since we was kids. Admittin' how she feels in public just isn't her way. Never has been." He shot me a wink. "Kinda reminds me of someone else I know."

At first I thought the "someone else" was Bonnie. Then I digested his words. He was hinting at me. "I share my feelings. Maybe not like other women do, but I still share them."

"No offense, darlin', but I've never met a woman who puts so much effort in keepin' a harness on things like you do."

My jaw tightened.

He playfully jabbed me in the side with his finger. "Now don't go all quiet on me with that pouty face of yours. I wasn't tryin' to offend. We've known each other long enough now to be honest with each other, wouldn't you say?"

"I guess so."

In an effort to ease the tension, get me talking again, he changed subjects. "There's somethin' else you should know about Grace. She may not like talkin' about herself, but she's one hell of a good listener."

"Meaning?"

"She's a therapist."

It explained a lot.

"As long as she doesn't try to shrink me, the two of us will get along just fine."

Cade looked outside, focused on the numbers displayed on the houses on our right. He stopped in front of one that displayed the numbers 399 vertically on wooden blocks. "Well, looks like we're here."

The globe-shaped porch light was lit, and a compact silver sedan was parked in the driveway, both positive signs of life inside. One step out of the car and the front door creaked open. A woman glanced out like she expected us, even though she couldn't have known we were coming. In a gesture of goodwill, and hoping to ease the nervousness manifested on her face, I smiled. She smiled back, but remained visibly alarmed nonetheless.

The woman's hair was long, dark, pinned into a loose bun below her left ear. I guesstimated her to be somewhere around forty years old, give or take, about the same age as I was. She wore a pair of black jeans, a white shirt, and a tan shawl. Simple. No socks, no shoes, no jewelry. Not even a wedding ring. Her eyes were dark and radiant, even though she looked fatigued.

"Ms. Kinkade," Cade said. "I'm Detective McCoy, and this is Detective Monroe. We're looking for your niece."

She pressed her palm to her chest. "Hannah? Why?"

"It's about the boy."

"Hannah's boyfriend? Daniel?"

Cade shook his head. "The baby, the one she gave up for adoption."

"Oh, no. Please don't bother her about the baby. She's been through so much already."

"We know," Cade said. "That's why it's important we talk to her."

"We're just trying to move on now. Besides, she hasn't done anything wrong."

"I never said she did."

"What other possible reason could you have to be here?"

"Renee, have you watched the news today?" I asked.

She shook her head. "Why?"

"You're not aware of what's happened?"

Her head sloped to one side. Confused. "Will one of you please tell me what's going on?"

"Finn is missing," I said.

"What do you mean *missing*? Have the Westwoods moved?"

"No. I mean to say he's been kidnapped."

Her eyelids fluttered open and closed at a rapid rate. She leaned against the door jamb for support. "When did this happen?"

"Last night," I said.

"Who took him, and why?"

"We don't know yet."

"What *do* you know?"

"Serena Westwood is dead."

Renee gasped, stepped back. She glanced down the hall, I assumed in the path of where Hannah was located. Renee either didn't know anything, or she was an expert at giving the appearance of innocence. She met my gaze, reduced her voice to a hush. "You don't think … you're not here because you think Hannah is involved somehow?"

"We just need to ask her a few questions," Cade said.

"She isn't … involved, I mean."

"Ma'am, can we come in?" Cade asked.

She hesitated.

"You know, I don't really enjoy being called ma'am. Do I look any older than the two of you?"

I had to say, I didn't blame her. The word made me cringe too.

"Fine," he said. "I'll stick to Ms. Kinkade then."

"Renee."

Was she stalling?

"I know you're worried about Hannah," Cade said. "All we need to do is verify her whereabouts last night, ask a few basic questions. It won't take long."

"There's no need. I can answer on Hannah's behalf. She was here, with me, all night."

"I appreciate you vouching for her. Either way, I'll need to talk to your niece."

Renee shook her head. "Hannah doesn't need to know about what's going on with the baby right now. Not yet. It's too much. Don't do this to her. Please."

"This isn't something you can keep from her," I said. "She's going to find out one way or another. And unfortunately, we might be the first to arrive at your house, but we won't be the last."

"I can't even get her to come out of her room. Maybe that's a good thing."

"And maybe it isn't," Cade said. "Let me ask you this … is there a television in her room?"

She shook her head.

"What about a laptop or a cell phone?"

Renee's eyes widened.

"It's already been on the news," Cade said. "And not just the local stations. If she's on the Facebooks or the Tweeter or whatever those teenage sites are called, she probably already knows."

Resisting the temptation to correct Cade wasn't easy. I found his lack of knowledge of social media charming. Renee mulled over his words then turned, scurrying down the hall. We followed. She reached a closed door, knocked. No answer.

"Hannah, honey," Renee said. "Can I talk to you for a minute?"

A faint groaning sound followed. "Aunt Ree, I'm tired. Can we talk later?"

Her voice was thin, delicate.

"It's important. I just need a few minutes, okay?"

Renee jiggled the handle. The door didn't open.

"Does she usually lock you out?" I asked, my voice lowered.

"Depends."

"On what?"

"The day. I've been trying to respect her privacy. She wasn't like this at first. I actually thought she'd get through it just fine. After Serena told her she couldn't see the baby again, she hasn't wanted to leave the bedroom."

"Do Hannah's parents know how withdrawn she's become? They weren't present when she had the baby, were they?"

Renee gnawed on her bottom lip, tensed at the mention of Hannah's parents. "We've ... ahh ... spoken a few times."

She was lying. Hannah's parents *didn't* know what was going on with their daughter, at least not all of it.

What reason would she have to keep it from them? And if Hannah was in such a bad place, why weren't they here supporting her?

Permission or not, Cade sized up the door, prepared to kick his way through it.

"Give me a minute first, will you?" I asked.

He wasn't thrilled, but he eased off. "If she suspects we're here, she could be out the window for all we know."

Renee turned up her nose. "Don't make assumptions. You don't know anything about her."

"Aunt Ree … who's out there with you?"

"Hannah? My name is Sloane Monroe. Can we talk?"

While I waited for a response, I assessed the door. It was bulky, made of solid wood, but the handle was another story, made of cheap, flimsy metal. I turned to Cade, silently mouthed the words "credit card." He took out his wallet, slid an American Express card onto my palm. Renee held her hand out in protest. Cade cinched a few fingers around her arm, escorted her a couple feet in the opposite direction.

It was just the two of us now, or it would be, if I could get inside.

"What do you want to talk about?" Hannah mumbled. "Why are you here?"

"Your baby. I know how hard it must be—what you're going through."

"You *know* how hard it is? Really? Have you ever done what I did?"

She had every right to be critical. I could have crossed my fingers, fudged the truth. I didn't. "No, never."

"Then you don't know anything."

I heard a shuffling sound on the other side of the door, and then she said, "Go way. Just leave me alone."

The words weren't yelled. They were barely even uttered. I'd maneuvered the card into the door twice without much luck. On the third try, the latch released and the door opened. I expected to be met with resistance, high-pitched screams of protest, similar to what I'd received in the past from girls her age. Hannah barely stirred, her body resting beneath several thick layers of bold-colored blankets. Her eyes peeked out, assessing me. They were blank, empty, devoid of life.

"Didn't I ask you to go away?" she stuttered. "No one ever listens to a word I say."

I sat at the edge of the bed, tried not to invade her personal space more than I already had. If I wanted her to talk, I needed to connect somehow. Confession time. "I had a miscarriage."

"What?"

Her attention was piqued. Good.

"Three of them, actually. I never had a baby because I couldn't have one."

She scooted into a semi-upright position, wadded up a pillow, tucked it behind her head. I considered it progress. A mass of wavy, blond locks trickled down her shoulders, tapering off at the waist. She was thin. Rail thin. And pale. Even in her dilapidated state, she was a beauty, exuding an angelic kind of childlike innocence. It was hard to believe she'd just had a baby when she was still a baby herself.

"So what, you're trying to adopt?" she asked. "You want to know stuff like why I chose the birth mother I did or something? You want advice? Did the agency send you here?"

"No."

"What then?" she asked.

"I just wanted you to know."

"Know what?"

"I can't empathize with the exact pain you're feeling, but I sympathize with your loss."

She removed the bundled-up covers, sat straight up, wrapped her arms around the front of her bent knees. "Guess so. I mean, it's not the same thing."

"I never said it was."

"What happened to you?"

"You mean why did I lose my children?"

She nodded.

"Depends on who you ask. I went to several different doctors, each one telling me they thought they could fix me, figure out the problem. They ran tests, but they couldn't find anything wrong. The man I was with at the time had fathered a child before, so it all came back to me. The last doctor I went to said I was just unlucky. I guess that's what a person says when they don't know what else *to* say. My grandmother said I was too skinny. My sister said I was too stressed. It's one of those topics people can't resist commenting on."

"Were you—stressed, I mean?"

"Were *you*?"

She nodded.

"And yet you delivered just fine," I said. "So do most teenage girls in your position. I wasn't too skinny. I was fit. I wasn't unhealthy either. I was conscious about the food I put into my body. In the end, it didn't matter. For whatever reason, my body rejected the idea of producing children."

"Did you … umm …"

Her eyes veered to the side.

"Whatever it is, it's all right. You can ask me."

"Did you name them, your babies, even though you never had them?"

"You know what? I've never told anyone this before, but I did."

"What were they—their names?"

"I never knew whether they were boys or girls; I lost them too soon to tell. If he was a boy, Lincoln, and if she was a girl, Isabella. What about you?"

"Logan." His name was whispered with gentle reverence, as if sacred. To her, it probably was.

"Logan's a beautiful name."

She met my gaze. "Why are you here, really?"

I felt wrong about being there. I wanted to back away, allow her to grieve. In my opinion, she didn't take Finn, and she probably didn't know who did. I knew that now. I saw no reason to increase her suffering. Maybe it was best she didn't know the truth. Not yet.

Renee entered the room, her face solemn. "Hannah, something's happened to Finn."

I shook my head, tried masking her words with my own. It was too late. The words rang out loud and clear, and Hannah soaked up every last one.

Hannah pitched the blankets to the side, stood. "What … did … you … say?"

"Renee," I said, "maybe it's best if we don't—"

"No. You two are right. Hannah needs to hear this."

"Hear what?" Hannah asked. "What's happening? Where is he? Where's my baby?!"

When Renee failed to respond, Hannah turned to me for answers.

I wanted to hit rewind, go back, give Hannah her baby, give Serena and Jack a different one. I couldn't help but wonder if this slight adjustment could have made all the difference.

Cade stepped around Renee, taking on Hannah himself in the gentlest way he knew how. "Hannah, last night Finn was kidnapped, and as of right now, he hasn't been found. Can you think of anyone who may have had a reason to abduct him—your boyfriend, or someone else who knows what you've been through?"

"She doesn't have a boyfriend," Renee said. "Not anymore."

"What about the birth father?" Cade asked.

"I don't see how that's possible," Renee said. "Daniel wasn't at the hospital when Hannah delivered. He never met the adoptive parents."

"How could this happen? Where were his …" Hannah choked on the words. "Where were Serena and Jack?"

"Jack was at work."

"And Serena?"

Renee spoke up. "I should be the one to tell her."

Hannah's eyes were wet, her cheeks stained with tears. "Tell me what, Ree?"

"Sweetie, Serena was killed last night."

"She's … dead?"

Hannah's legs wobbled beneath her, unable to sustain her frail weight. I grappled for her arm and missed. Hannah stretched out a hand, reached for Renee, and collapsed.

CHAPTER 13

Light flickered in and out of the room as a log cracked, relaxing into the embers skirting it on all sides. I stared into the fire, sipped chamomile tea. My thoughts centered on the visit with Hannah a couple hours before. She'd fainted, blacked-out. Not for long, just long enough to scare Renee into accepting a harsh reality—her niece needed help—the kind she wasn't qualified to give.

After Hannah came to, her aunt drove her to the hospital. Renee called an hour later saying Hannah had been diagnosed with severe malnutrition. The doctor on call admitted her, said he'd like to keep her overnight, maybe longer. Renee blamed herself. She felt she should have noticed sooner, done more to help. I disagreed. Hannah was old enough to take responsibility for her own actions. It was up to her now.

"You okay?"

Cade's question was simple, but not one I could answer.

I abandoned my thoughts, watched him cross the room, sit beside me.

"Your house," I said, "it's nice. The last time I was here you hadn't decided what you were doing yet."

"With the job promotion and Shelby finally takin' to the place, I figured it was time we settle down, make a go of it. I have to admit, it feels good to be back."

"You grew up here, but Shelby wasn't raised here, right?"

"My ex, Shelby's mom, was never big on Jackson Hole. She couldn't appreciate the beauty of it all. She wanted different. Different town, different life. So I gave it to her. And when that wasn't enough, she decided different meant she needed a new man. Lookin' back now, I never should have agreed to leave this place."

I wanted to entwine my arm in his, bury my head in his shoulder. I didn't. I held back like I always did, fearing what might happen if I acted on one non-work-related impulse for once. I used my words, hoping they'd express the same form of comfort that physical affection did. I wasn't foolish enough to believe they would. For now, in this moment, they were all I had to give.

"I can't count all the things in my life I'd go back and change if I could," I said. "I make sense of it all by telling myself it's never too late to start again, to create the life I've always wanted. I'm trying to figure it out. Someday I will."

"I don't want to pain you by bringin' up a sore subject, so if I'm out of line here, feel free to slug me if you want."

"Whatever it is, tell me."

"I overheard your conversation with Hannah earlier. Is it true, what you said?"

"About the babies?"

He nodded.

My throat felt tight, like someone had clasped hold of my neck with their husky, fat fingers and squeezed. "Every word."

"When my wife took off a few years back, left me, left our daughter, I thought I knew what it meant to suffer. When I look at you, I realize you've lost so much more than I ever have."

A sister. A father. A mother. A grandfather. A friend. My babies. Bits and pieces of myself along the way. Death was a special kind of desolation I couldn't seem to escape.

"You have your cross to bear and I have mine. We all do."

"I'm sorry you suffered somethin' no woman should have to endure. Seein' you with Shelby, knowin' how much she admires you. I have no doubt you would have been a wonderful mother."

I fisted my hand around the handle of the mug, relocated the rush of emotions pooling inside. If I was blessed with a daughter, she would have been close to Shelby's age now. "It was a long time ago. When I look back, it doesn't seem real. It's like it happened to another woman in another life, a life I wasn't meant to lead."

I set the mug down. Honed in on it. Honed in on the flecks in the carpet—mixtures of black, copper, and gold. I would have focused on anything, as long as it wasn't him. Expressing myself made me feel vulnerable and weak, even though I'd come to trust him.

He stretched out his hand, hooked it around mine, his thumb massaging my palm. "I don't know what happened. The last time I saw you, you seemed fine. After I left, we spoke on the phone a handful of times, but it wasn't the same. You were different."

"Different, how?"

"Not sure I know the right words, exactly. Quiet and unresponsive, I s'pose. I could tell somethin' wasn't right. It still isn't."

"I was fine," I said. "I'm fine now."

Maybe if I kept saying it, one day, I would be.

"If you don't want to be here, if I'm pushin' you by askin' for your help, you don't have to stay."

I took the case. I accepted it. I was fine. Maybe not completely, but I was coping at least. What more did he want from me?

"I'm staying."

"It's just—harder to have you here than I thought it would be."

The obvious thing for me to ask next was *why.* There was no need. I knew why. Somehow I thought if I focused on Finn, if I shut up about discussing the likelihood of whether something was happening between us, he would too. I wasn't dealing with the average guy. This was Cade. The I'm-not-afraid-to-get-right-to-the-point guy. My equal in so many ways.

"I want to be part of your life, Sloane. But I won't force you to be part of mine."

"I *am* in your life. I'm right here."

His palm was still pressed over mine, his grip tight, obstructing the flow of blood to my hand. I almost pulled away.

"We're friends," he continued. "I thought it would be enough. I convinced myself I could be around you and keep my feelings for you under control. Seein' you, touchin' you—I can't."

"Do you want me to go?" I asked.

"This isn't about stayin' or goin'. It's about me wanting more. I'm askin' you to open up, to trust me. I don't know if you want me and you just need more time, or if you don't and you never will. Either way, I can't go another day without puttin' my intentions on the table. I won't lie to you, and I won't lie to myself. Wouldn't be right."

"I care for you, Cade. You know I do, don't you?"

"Care for me how exactly? As a friend, more than a friend?"

"Please don't push me to have this conversation right now," I said. "I'm not saying we can't have it, or we won't have it. I'm just asking you to let it sit, for now. Can you?"

When he didn't respond, I did the one thing I was hoping to avoid. I gazed at his face, even though I knew how arduous it would be for me to deny my feelings once I did. There was something about him—something so refreshingly rare, so raw—something I felt the first day we met and had always resisted. It was the exact reason why we were right here, right now, having this conversation. The worst part of all? *He knew.*

I speculated Cade had sensed my feelings all along, sensed things I wasn't even aware I was feeling, things I wouldn't allow myself to feel. My mind had been blocked, safeguarded by a solid, black blindfold of truth. All I wanted was to be in the moment, *this* moment. Cade wasn't the only one who wanted to know my true feelings, *I* wanted to know. In order to make that discovery, I'd have to strip away the fear, let everything else go.

Cade rose to his feet, pulling me up with him. He freed my hand, and I felt the blood rush back again. He cupped my face in his hands, smiled down at me.

"Are you leaving?" I asked.

"It's late. I'm tired."

"You don't have to go. Stay. We'll talk about the case, make a game plan, decide what we're doing tomorrow. We can do that, can't we?"

He entwined his hands around my waist, pulled me close. "I want someone to share my life with— someone by my side. I'm ready, Sloane. You're not, or you haven't decided you are, at least. So I'm gonna do what's right and let you come to me. We can work together, and we can remain friends. But as far as I'm concerned, you're the woman for me."

I stared into his eyes thinking how freeing it must be to shed the layers of insecurity, take risks without the promise of affection being returned.

Cade bent down, his lips gently brushing across my neck. "Now you know my intentions, what's in my heart."

He let go.

Left the room.

Left me standing alone.

More alone than I'd felt in a really long time.

CHAPTER 14

I slept exactly one hour and twenty minutes that night. During the remaining hours, I wrestled the thoughts I had of Cade out of my head and tried concentrating on Hannah, Finn, Jack—anything and everything having to do with the crime. My efforts were admirable, except when I closed my eyes, I saw Cade. When I opened them, I saw Cade. He was the reflection in the window, in the mirror, in my mind—a holographic image flicking off and on like a broken projection machine.

Finally even my brain reached overload, and Cade was put to the side, if only for a short hour and twenty minutes. He'd have to wait. We had a baby to find.

A note scribbled in Cade's handwriting on the door of the refrigerator the next morning let me know he'd gone out for a while. It didn't say where or when he expected to return. The note was signed with the letter C and a rather crazed-looking smiley face with a peanut-shaped head and one eyeball three times larger than the other one. I took it as a positive sign, hoping he wasn't too thwarted by my inability to return his feelings the previous night.

Shelby had already left for school, which meant I had the house to myself. The blissful solitude lasted ten short minutes before the doorbell chimed. I cruised to the bathroom, cringing when I glanced at myself in the mirror. My pixie-cut hairstyle didn't fare so well pre-shower. With two-inch pieces shooting in every direction, I looked more porcupine than human. My mascara had also smeared, creating an off-putting charcoal affect around my brown, doe-shaped eyes. Perhaps porcupine wasn't the right word. I looked a bit more *Close Encounters of the Third Kind*.

During the brief assessment of myself, the doorbell was pressed two or three more times. Apparently patience was a virtue the person on the outside didn't possess. I abandoned any inkling of fixing the unfixable and approached the door, sneaking in a quick look-see through the peephole first. The gesture didn't go unnoticed and was met with an immediate, "Hey! I can see you. Cade? Shelby? Open the door."

The woman between myself and several layers of wood had a mass of wavy, caramel-colored locks with random strands of white highlights. The wavy mass framed her face, making it impossible for me to get a good look at her. I guessed she was another relative of Cade's. The town seemed inundated with members of the McCoy clan in one capacity or another.

I cracked the door open and peeked out, not wanting to frighten the woman away, not wanting to give the impression I'd allow her inside either. She saw it as an opportunity, applying pressure to the wood with her hand, flinging the door open all the way.

The woman took in my unkempt appearance, snickered, and said, "What happened to you?"

Nice opener. It had a "we'll never be friends" ring to it.

"Long night," I said.

"Who are you, and why are you in Cade's house? This *is* Cade's new house, isn't it?"

I detected a hint of an accent in her voice. Southern maybe. The woman was dressed in a spaghetti-strapped tank top and a skirt that was hanging on for dear life. Maybe she'd never heard of safety pins, or a sewing machine, or smaller clothes. Or maybe she was short on money, along with a handful of other virtues like civility and respect.

It was possible we were the same age, although time hadn't extended the same kindness to her that it had to me. She had three tattoos, visible ones anyway. A star, a rose, and some cursive words on her inner arm inked in a foreign language. Her unique packaging caught my eye almost as much as the two bags of luggage resting at her feet did. Whoever she was, she'd come prepared for a lengthy stay at Casa de McCoy.

"Before we get to who I am," I said, "I'd like to know who you are first."

She slouched, flattened a hand over her hip. "Fine by me. I'm a friend of Serena's. I'm here for her funeral … and whatever else comes of my being here. I got my bags, so I can stay for a while."

I got my bags? Poor grammar aside, there was a gleam in her eye when she said it. Her agenda may have started with a plan to attend Serena's funeral, but it ended somewhere else. I was curious about what it had to do with her choosing Cade's house to squat at in the meantime.

"You're early," I said. "Serena's funeral isn't until the day after tomorrow."

"That's okay. Like I said, I'm here. Maybe for good."

The longer our conversation lasted, the more I wanted her to leave.

"You never gave me your name."

"Oh, right. It's Wendy."

"Wendy … ?"

"Let's say McCoy for now."

Perfect. She *was* related. Most likely the black sheep of the McCoy family.

"How do you know Cade?" I asked.

"You're in his house, and you don't know?"

"If I did, I wouldn't be asking."

"I'm his wife."

I pressed a hand against the wall, steadied myself, realizing my assumption of who she was had been way off. After Cade's confession the night before, seeing the woman he'd been married to for so many years was unexpected. He swore Wendy was gone, out of his life forever, and yet here she was on his doorstep.

"Wife? Current or ex? From what I gather, Cade doesn't have a wife. Not anymore."

She exhaled enough air to qualify her for a medal in free-range cow tipping. "Legally, well … on paper, I'm his ex. For now. What's it to you?"

What *was* it to me? Good question. Either way, Cade meant a lot to me. She meant nothing. She'd shit all over him and Shelby. If she was back for seconds, she had to go.

"Does Cade know you're coming?" I asked. "Does he know you're here?"

She mused for a moment, daydreamed, like she'd played out the moment they came together again over and over in her mind.

"He will soon enough. I wanted it to be a surprise."

Oh, it was going to be a surprise all right.

"So you're what—here to win him back?"

She clicked her black, pointy boot on the redwood planks a few times before swishing a finger in front of my face in an S pattern. "You know what, I don't think I like the way you're talking to me. Just who are you?"

"My name's Sloane, and what you like or don't like doesn't concern me."

"Huh. Never heard of you. So *you* don't concern me either."

"How could you hear of me?" I asked. "You ditched your family a few years ago. You have no idea what their life is like now. Nor should you."

"I have a few friends here. I've stayed apprised of Cade's life."

Big word for such an unsophisticated person.

Show off.

"What about your daughter's life? After you abandoned her, did you stay *apprised* of her life too?"

She depressed her eyelids into tiny slits. "Don't act like you know anything about me *or* my family."

Knowing the war of words would continue for an unforeseeable amount of time, I opted out, choosing the path of least resistance. It was early, and I didn't have my filter on yet. "Cade's not here. I'll tell him you stopped by."

I stepped back, pushed the door forward. She wedged her hand inside, jamming it so it couldn't close.

"I'll wait," she spat.

"Not in here, you won't."

"This isn't your house. You can't tell me—"

"It isn't yours either. Since I'm the one on the inside and you're not, I get to make the decision."

Her finger was twirling in the breeze again. I stared at it, thought about how easy it would be for me to grab the digit, snap it back. It halted in midair when she heard Cade's Dodge Ram crunch up the drive. The truck came to a halt behind a trio of stately pines. The truck door rocked open and he stepped out, a drink gripped in each hand.

I stepped outside, and knowing there wasn't anything more I could do to prevent this moment from happening, I waited for the showdown to begin. Cade glanced at the two of us standing side by side on the porch. He jolted back like someone had zapped his chest with a taser gun. Since her visit was unexpected, I presumed his internal system was going haywire. His face revealed a combination of expired emotions—pain, frustration, anger. I wanted to save him from reopening his healed wounds. I couldn't. I couldn't do anything except stand there and watch it all unravel.

Cade's eyes locked on Wendy, and she seized her moment. "Hi, honey. Long time. It's good to see you again. I've missed you."

Honey? I wanted to gag.

One of the drinks toppled from his hand, the lid busting off as liquid sloshed all over the ground.

Wendy tried taking a step forward. Her misguided plan to launch herself into Cade's arms was halted when the toe of her boot caught on the front of my foot, and she was thrust to the ground instead. Her knees hit first, scraping along the wood as she went down. She tossed her head toward me, her eyes screaming all the things her lips couldn't say—not in front of Cade.

I remained neutral on the outside while internally savoring my perfectly executed sabotage. Wendy used the unfortunate event to her advantage, stretching an arm toward Cade, prompting him to come to her rescue. He walked past her, caught my hand in his as he entered the house, and kicked the door closed, leaving her on the front porch. Alone.

"Cade, if you need some time with her," I said, "I can leave for a while, give the two of you a chance to talk."

"There's nothin' to talk about."

"She seems to think there is."

"Look, I need you to know somethin'—I don't know what she said to you before I arrived, but I didn't invite her here, and I don't want her here. I didn't know she was comin', okay?"

"Okay."

"Truly, if I had known, if I'd had any idea she—"

"Cade, it's okay. I'm fine. Everything's all right."

He inserted the paper cup he was holding into my hand. "Here."

"What's this?"

"Peace offerin'. I wanted to apologize about last night. I got a couple drinks in me and allowed the liquid courage to take over. I knew you weren't ready. I shouldn't have pushed. Won't happen again, I promise."

"Cade, you didn't do anything wrong. You don't need to—"

The front door blew open.

"We need to talk," Wendy interrupted.

Cade pointed at the door. "Get. Out."

Wendy flashed a snarky glance at me that said "watch this." She marched up to Cade like she owned him. Her knee was bleeding. Not a lot, just enough to show her fall had inflicted a minor amount of damage. I shouldn't have been pleased with myself for aiding in her misfortune, but I couldn't help it. I wanted her gone.

"I'm not leaving here until I say what I came to say," Wendy said. "So tell your little friend here to give us some privacy so the two of us can work things out."

Cade snatched Wendy's arm with so much force I thought it might snap off. He escorted her to the door, flung her back outside. "We're over, Wendy. We've been over for a long time. I don't need you. Shelby doesn't need you. Don't you *ever* come here again."

To make his point clear, he grabbed her bags and hurled them off the porch. One of the bags opened, shooting bits of clothing through the air. Wendy stared at Cade in disbelief. It wasn't what she expected. Wasn't the reunion she'd drilled into her mind. She gathered her things, shoved them inside a beat-up, two-door coupe, and flipped me the bird all the way out of the driveway.

Whatever this was and whatever her reasons were for being here—I had the distinct feeling it wasn't over.

CHAPTER 15

I sat with Cade in the parking lot in front of Grand Memorial Hospital. We parked. He didn't get out. He leaned forward, tapped his thumb on the steering wheel. Unsure of what he might say, I absorbed the quiet. Waited.

"You haven't said a word to me since this mornin'," he said. "If there's anything you want to talk to me about or ask me, you can."

"I know."

"Wanna tell me what's botherin' you?"

Not really. I had a feeling I was about to anyway, but I thought I'd try a more evasive approach first.

"If you're thinking I'm upset about your ex-wife showing up, I'm not," I said.

"Well, somethin's wrong. If you don't tell me, I'll just keep guessin' what it is. I know you like to keep things to yourself. You're a proud woman. Keepin' things quiet doesn't just affect you though, it affects everyone around you."

He was right, of course. And I knew it. I'd always known.

"I've been thinking about Finn, wondering where he might be, hoping we still have a chance to bring him back to Jack alive. No matter what else is going on right now, that boy is my priority. Our priority. Everything else can wait."

It wasn't what he expected me to say. The answer was safe. It was also true. It just wasn't the only thing on my mind.

"We'll find him," he said. "I know we will."

I'd successfully diverted. I was in the safe zone. The topic could have ended right there, if only my true feelings, the ones stowed deep inside my soul, hadn't bubbled over. I had no choice, no control, which wasn't like me. I switched gears.

"I get the feeling Wendy wants to be part of your life again."

His playful smile let me know he knew there was more I wanted to say.

"Don't matter. It's too late."

"What if she wants to see Shelby? Will you allow it?"

"Shelby's almost a grown woman. I'll tell her the truth about what happened today. Let her decide."

Even so, he was worried. I could tell.

"Wendy's … different than I expected," I said.

"I almost didn't recognize her myself. She used to be—I don't quite know the right word—softer, I guess. Now she's looks rough, like she's aged ten years in the three since I saw her last."

"What do you think happened?"

"Who knows? The guy she took off with—he's the possessive, dominating type. I imagine she spent most of her time tryin' to live up to his unrealistic expectations. And now he's either thrown her out and she's been replaced, or she ran. Hard to tell. Either way, not my problem. I'm not some fallback she can run to after everything's gone wrong. She made her choice."

"Was she really friends with Serena?" I asked.

"A long time ago. Serena never said anything to me about stayin' in touch over the years. Guess it's possible."

"What about your family?"

Admit it or not, I knew I was pushing the "nosy" boundary. I didn't care.

"She's never been close to anyone in my immediate family. When we married, they accepted her, included her, did whatever they could to help her fit in.

In the end, she did everything she could to push them all away."

"I wonder if anyone else knows she's here," I said.

"Doubt it. She's not welcome, and if she tries to stay, she'll learn a harsh lesson real quick."

"If Wendy wants to be a part of Shelby's life now, and Shelby agrees, what will you—"

"Not gonna happen, Sloane. Wendy lives for one person and one person only. Herself. As for her intentions with me, I may forgive, I may even try to forget, but I'll never go back. What's done is done. She has no place in my life now."

He glanced out the window, a wide grin on his face like he was curbing an unquenchable desire to burst out laughing.

"What?" I asked.

"I saw what you did earlier, stickin' your foot out there so she'd trip over it."

I pulled on the truck's handle, hopped out, looked away so he wouldn't catch me reliving the glorious moment yet again. "I have no idea what you're talking about. I can't help it if the woman didn't watch where she was stepping."

He tipped his cowboy hat toward me, winked. "If you say so."

CHAPTER 16

While Cade spoke to Renee in the waiting area, I found Hannah's room. An older man who looked to be somewhere in the almost-fifty range hunched over Hannah's bed, spewing sentences at such a rapid rate, even I couldn't make sense of what he was saying. He enunciated some of his words more than the others, allowing me to catch bits and pieces here and there:

"How could you embarrass your mother and embarrass me …"

"No daughter of mine …"

"After all we've done …"

"You're nothing but a selfish, stupid …"

A crippling look of fear and helplessness was reflected on Hannah's innocent face. Her head remained upright, unmoved. Her eyes shifted toward me as the word "bitch" rolled off the man's tongue.

For me, it was an "oh, hell no" moment. I'd heard enough. I knocked on the wall inside the room to get the man's attention. "Excuse me."

The man stopped midsentence, circled his body around, faced me. His head was round and perfect, like a plate that had been molded by hand. His eyes were something else entirely. They were narrow and cruel, devoid of compassion.

On the opposite side of the room, a feeble-looking woman sat in a chair, her eyes fastened on her hands loosely placed on her lap. She swayed, rocking back and forth like she was in a trance. She stopped for a moment, wiped the clear moisture that dripped from one of her eyes, and went back to rocking again.

The man stood, all five-foot-nothing inches of him, feet shoulder-width apart, fists clenched in front of him like he was the goalie and I was the puck.

Let the sparring begin.

"And you are?" he growled.

"Do you always speak to your daughter that way?" I asked.

"Do *you* always get involved in issues that aren't your business?"

I advanced to Hannah's bed, set a vase of pastel daisies on a nightstand. The level of discomfort he displayed—in the form of wild, flailing hand gestures—heightened once I reached her.

No matter.

He didn't intimidate me.

He infuriated me.

Big difference.

"I came by to see how you're doing," I said to Hannah. "Cade's here too. He just stopped in the lobby for a minute to talk to your aunt."

"I'm fine," she whispered.

She wasn't fine. She was terrified.

"Who are you, and why are you here?" the man demanded. "What's your angle?"

"My *angle*?"

"Whoever you are, it's not possible you know my daughter well. If you did, I'd know you. So don't waltz in here pretending like you care for her wellbeing."

"You don't know me. So don't pretend you know who I am or how I feel."

The man yanked on my wrist, an obvious lapse in judgment. "If you need something, you can address *me*, not her."

I wrenched my wrist free of his sweaty grip, issued a warning. "Don't *ever* lay a hand on me again."

My words fell flat, meant nothing. I didn't expect them to. The way he verbally attacked Hannah coupled with the obvious fear displayed from the woman I assumed was his wife—he didn't just demean women, he didn't respect them either.

"I'm Hannah's father, Aaron. What is it you think you need from my daughter? I'll ask you again. Why are you here?"

"I'm not here to see you, and I'm not here to talk with you, either. What I came to say is for Hannah's benefit, not yours. So if you'll excuse me—"

"Since I'm Hannah's parent and you're not, whatever you came to say is my business."

"Is Hannah incapable of speaking for herself?" I turned to the woman. "And you—do you ever stand up for your daughter, or do you do what you're doing now and let her fend for herself?"

The woman's eyes bulged.

"Now wait just a—" the man started.

I held a finger in the air, stopping him. I turned toward Hannah. "If there's anything you need, even if you just want to talk, I want you to call me. Anytime, day or night. Okay?" Knowing where my number would end up if I gave it to her in front of her father, I added, "Your aunt knows how to reach me."

"I'm … umm … fine."

She was like a wind-up toy. Turn the dial and hear the same prerecorded words, over and over again. I didn't want to leave her, but since I was a few seconds away from being escorted from the room, I knew I couldn't stay.

I leaned in close, talked in her ear. "I have a few errands to run. I'll be back to check on you later."

"No," Hannah begged. "Please don't."

I entwined her hand in mine. "I'll see you soon. Don't worry. Everything's going to be okay."

A tear rolled down her cheek. She looked at her father then at me. "No, it isn't. Not anymore."

"What's that, Hannah?" Aaron demanded. "What are you saying to this woman?"

"Nothing," I responded. "She didn't say anything."

"Your name," Aaron demanded. "You haven't given it to me."

I crossed in front of him, stopped at the door. "If I felt like giving it to you, I would have."

I left the room, keenly aware of the weighty thud of Aaron's footsteps trailing behind, waiting to get me into the hall so he could threaten me, or worse. The movement stopped when I walked out, saw Cade waiting in the hallway. Apparently dominating women was more Aaron's style. Men were another story.

"How's she doing?" Cade asked.

I cast my eyes toward Hannah's room, watched Aaron slink back inside.

I steered Cade the opposite way. "Where's Renee?"

"She hasn't left the waiting room. Why? What's wrong?"

"Everything."

I charged down the hall, surveyed the groups of people, sitting, waiting to be called. I pinpointed Renee, her eyes glued to a page in a book. I took hold of her arm, yanking her out of the raggedy chair she sat in.

"What is it?" she asked. "What's happened?"

"We need to talk. Now."

CHAPTER 17

"What the hell is going on, Renee?!" I snapped.

A mother sitting beside two young teens flashed me a disparaging look. I mouthed a sincere "oops, sorry" in her direction. If I was going to vent, we needed privacy.

"Let's meet back at your house," I said. "We can talk there."

She sat, stone-faced, fingers massaging her temples. "No … please."

"Why not?"

"I don't want to leave Hannah. I *can't* leave her—not right now."

"Stay or go," I said. "Either way, you better start talking."

"What am I missin'?" Cade cut in. "What's happened?"

I looked at Renee. "Do you want to tell him or shall I?"

She bent down, rested her elbows on her pant legs. "Not here."

The three of us regrouped in a darkened room in an unused wing of the hospital.

"I can't stay long," Renee said.

"I agree," I said. "Hannah needs to be protected. Why aren't you with her now?"

"Aaron won't let me anywhere near her. Not after what I…"

I gave her a moment to recover, to finish what she intended to say. The words dissolved, evaporating into the air around us.

"Her parents didn't know she was pregnant, did they?" I asked.

"I hid it from them, it's true."

"How's that even possible?" I asked. "She can't be more than a size three."

Renee straddled a chair, pulled on her shirt several times like she was trying to fan herself off. "Last year Hannah came to stay with me for part of her summer break. While she was here, she met Daniel, the baby's father. They dated for a while. She left, returned to Idaho to finish her senior year of high school. Around Thanksgiving, Aaron decided he wanted to spend the holiday on a cruise ship instead of celebrating with family. He sent Hannah to my house while they were away."

"I'm guessing that's when Hannah rekindled things with Daniel and got pregnant," I said.

Cade shook his head, his face grim, disgusted, most likely thinking of how he'd feel if it had been his own daughter.

"You're right," Renee said. "She did get pregnant. I didn't even know she'd slept with the guy until late one night in January. Hannah called me. She was frantic. She'd taken three pregnancy tests. All of them positive, with a big, pink plus sign."

"So the two of you came up with a plan that didn't involve telling her parents."

"You don't get the point."

"Oh, I believe I do," I said. "And I'm not blaming you. I've just met Aaron, and I can see why you did it. But you should have explained everything to me when we were at your house last night."

"What difference does it make now? You're looking for Hannah's baby. I don't see what your investigation has to do with the choice we made."

"Maybe you're right. But what if you're wrong?"

"I don't see how I could be."

"Only three percent of children under the age of five are killed at the hand of a stranger. The other ninety-seven percent are fathers, mothers, relatives, and acquaintances. Bottom line—in a case like this, it almost always comes back to someone who knew the child. And guess what? Since this was a semi-open adoption, with exception to Jack and Serena and their family, most people didn't know. That fact alone narrows the potential suspect field quite a bit, wouldn't you say?"

"My brother didn't do it. He wasn't aware the baby existed."

"How can you be sure?" I questioned. "He doesn't strike me as the kind of man that lets things slip by him."

"If you would have been around today when he found out, you would have seen the genuine shock on his face. All he's done since he arrived is tear her apart, interrogate her. He demanded to know why Hannah hadn't aborted the baby when she had the chance. He wouldn't have wanted her to keep it, he would have wanted her to get rid of it. He's glad the child's gone."

"You said he interrogated Hannah. About what?"

"The names of anyone who knew about the baby."

"Why does it matter so much to him?" I asked. "The baby isn't part of her life anymore."

"There's nothing my brother values more than his reputation."

"Meaning he'd go to any lengths to protect it," I said.

"Not by stealing a baby. He doesn't kill, he controls … everything. Hannah was suffocating under his roof. Part of me thinks she even planned the pregnancy."

"Why? What was she hoping to achieve?"

"She wanted to run away, disown her parents, and raise the baby on her own. It took months for me to talk her out of it. Finally, I convinced her to think of the child, to put the child's needs above her own. Moving here, with me, getting her first shot of freedom, *real* freedom, I didn't want her to drop out of college and forsake a life she hadn't even started."

Cade leaned forward, reclined his arms on his knees. "So, how did it work—your plan?"

"Hannah continued to live at home with her parents. She hid the pregnancy until she finished her senior year."

"How is that possible?" I asked.

"Baggy shirts mostly, hoodies. Even when she was nine months along, she wasn't very big."

"And you're telling us no one noticed?"

"Hannah's always dressed that way, so it wasn't much of a red flag. Aaron was too preoccupied with his own life, and Ann is so timid. Even if she thought twice about it, I doubt she would have said anything. She's not a 'rock the boat' kind of person."

She wasn't a *person* at all. She was an obedient robot.

"What about Hannah's friends?" I asked.

"I'm not sure. If anyone else knew, they never said anything. As soon as Hannah graduated, I invited her here for the summer. She told her parents she wanted to live with me while attending the university in Jackson Hole. Aaron agreed as long as she lived under my roof, and she enrolled."

"But she never went."

"I didn't know she was going to fall apart until after the baby was born. She couldn't function, let alone start college. I thought I'd wait it out, give her some time to heal. I hoped I could talk her into trying again the following semester."

"Were her parents aware she never started school?" I asked.

"Do you know how many times they've been to see Hannah since she moved here in May?" She curled her fingers into a circle. "Zero. Aaron called every night, thinking he was keeping tabs on her via phone, and he sent money every other week. He asked about her grades, and we found a way to work around it so he wouldn't suspect anything was wrong."

I didn't even want to know.

"Now they're here," I said. "They know she lied, they know *you* lied. What happens next?"

"Aaron hasn't let her out of his sight. I'm worried."

Renee had come clean about one issue and skirted the other. Either she didn't know what her brother was capable of, or she feigned ignorance. I wanted to believe she knew. Abusers don't wake up one day as adults and turn into someone they never were before.

"The abuse," I said. "How bad is it?"

"Abuse?" Cade raised a brow, looked at me, looked at Renee. "What abuse?"

"You mean verbal?" Renee asked.

"I mean—when was the last time Aaron physically abused his wife or his daughter?"

She shifted on her seat, thwarting my accusation. "Are you serious? He would never—"

"Oh, come on, Renee. You can't expect me to believe it's never happened before."

"I don't know what you're suggesting. My brother may be a lot of things, but to allege he'd harm his own family?"

"Open your eyes," I said. "See your brother for who he truly is. It's about time, don't you think?"

Cade turned toward me. "Why are you so sure there's been abuse?"

He wasn't second-guessing my assessment. He was clarifying, getting the facts straight before he decided the best way to handle the situation.

"I looked Hannah's mother in the eye not thirty minutes ago," I said. "Her behavior, her inability to make eye contact, the way she recoiled when Aaron took the slightest step toward her—I'm telling you Cade, she's a battered woman."

"Did you see any bruises on her?" he asked.

"She was covered up. Almost too covered up."

He nodded. "I believe you."

"I don't," Renee said.

"Then you're a fool," I said.

And a liar. Over the last couple minutes, she'd nibbled at the inside of her cheek like she was trying to chomp right through it.

"You'd better start believing," I said. "If he's as mad as you say he is, Hannah shouldn't be left alone with him."

"Why do you think I haven't left yet?" Renee asked.

I looked at Cade. "What can you do—anything?"

"Not much unless the wife or the daughter comes forward. Until then, as far as the law is concerned, my hands are tied."

CHAPTER 18

Cade's hands may have been tied when it came to involving his fellow men at arms, but it didn't mean he wasn't prepared to lean on Aaron a little, or a lot, depending on the way you looked at it. Renee returned to her post, vowing to keep us updated, and to remain by Hannah's side until she was released.

Cade and I found our way back to room 211. We'd just about reached the entrance when a man dressed in scrubs stopped us. "Are you family? Because if you're not, I'm sorry, but I can't permit you access to the patient's room."

Cade stepped in front of me, acknowledging the male nurse with a single tip of his cowboy hat.

"I'm Detective McCoy, and this is Detective Monroe. We just need to look in on the girl, make sure she's all right."

"Sir, I can't allow you to—"

Cade flashed his badge. "We *will* be lookin' in on the girl. Step aside."

So much for Aaron's attempt to keep me at bay.

Cade entered the room, acknowledged Hannah's mother first. "Ma'am."

Her eyes flashed, darted around, never resting on any one thing. Aaron vaulted off the chair he was sitting in, his face puffed up like a cobra ready to strike.

"You again. There has to be some kind of security in this hospital." He turned to his wife. "Where's my phone?"

"Mr. Kinkade. My name is Cade McCoy."

Aaron snatched the phone from his wife's outstretched hand. "Yeah, what's it to me?"

Cade flashed his badge a second time. "I need you to step outside."

"What for?"

"We need to talk."

"About?"

"It would be better if we had this conversation in private," Cade said.

"I'm not going anywhere. I know what this is. You're trying to get me out of the room so *she* can put the wrong kind of ideas into my daughter's head."

She meaning me.

"This isn't about Hannah, Mr. Kinkade. It's about you."

"Doesn't matter. I'm staying."

"I'd rather not do this in front of the ladies," Cade stated. "So I'll ask one last time."

"Do what in front of who?"

Aaron held steady in his position, didn't budge.

"Explain what will happen if you ever lay a finger on your wife or daughter again."

Ann stiffened. Hannah looked right at me, her eyes telling a story words wouldn't allow. My hunch was right.

Aaron's face inflamed, turning a radish-like shade of red. Through clenched teeth he managed to serve up a few garbled words. "You don't know what you're talking—"

"I'm not gonna stand here and debate the facts," Cade said coolly. "You've been warned. I'm extendin' you a one-time, one-chance offer. If you value your life, you'll take it."

CHAPTER 19

I'd never been the kind of person who placed blame on problems I considered my own, but if I had to blame someone, I suppose I'd condemn society for driving me inside, shutting me away for all those months. Seeking shelter from the outside world hadn't been such a bad thing. It kept me away from the news, away from hearing about the latest shooting in an unsavory part of town, the drunk driver who plowed through a mother and child in the crosswalk. The world was filled with it. Sin. Crime. Corruption. Lies. Enough noise to make a person want to dig their own grave and bury themselves nice and deep.

My grandmother's intervention hauled me out of the fortress I'd built to keep me inside and humanity out. She gave me hope, purpose, the will to try again, to find meaning and purpose in my life. I longed for it, desperately. But it was times like this, days like today, when I was willing to abandon it all, retreat to a safe place within.

A phone call from Maddie after I left the hospital with Cade shed light on the real story behind what happened to the baby boy found dead inside the duffel bag on a long stretch of Utah highway. A woman had come forward claiming to be the deceased infant's mother. She was penniless, and without a job, money, or any relatives to rely on, she'd convinced herself she wouldn't be able to give birth at the hospital the way everyone else did. Instead, she elected to have the child herself at home. Assisting with the delivery was her current boyfriend, a man who wasn't the child's biological father. They were no experts, but hell, they were confident they could get the job done. After all, they'd prepared for the event by watching several home-birth videos on the Internet. And if that doesn't say "you can do it yourself," nothing does, right?

All was lost when the baby arrived stillborn, a result of the woman's umbilical cord developing a tight knot. The child had suffered from a loss of oxygen, something that may have been prevented had the mother been under the care of a proper physician. The bruises the baby sustained were postmortem, an unfortunate result of mother and boyfriend playing

God, thinking they could revive the boy, bring him back to life.

Swaddling the dead child in her arms as she became aware nothing she could do would save him, the mother had panicked. The boyfriend consoled her, said not to worry, he'd "take care of it." He left the apartment, returning an hour later, unwilling to discuss the exact details of the baby's whereabouts. The woman confessed she had no idea what her boyfriend had done with the dearly departed until she clicked on the television, hearing the sordid details unfold on the news.

When the boyfriend was questioned about why he hadn't just placed the baby in a dumpster, he said the way he saw it, if the wee one was found, the state would make sure the infant had a proper burial, something the boyfriend felt the child deserved. And what better place for a dead child to get noticed than the shoulder of a well-traveled freeway?

What an unbelievably screwed-up world.

CHAPTER 20

"What can you tell me about the way Serena died?" Cade asked.

A coroner Cade referred to as "Hooker" stood a few feet away, his hand resting on the edge of a metallic table that contained Serena Westwood's body. Hooker was tall, about six foot five. He had ginger-colored hair and an adorable, crooked smile that brightened a room even as gloomy as the one we were standing in.

"I thought you were ordered off this case," Hooker lectured Cade.

From his tone of voice, we were about to get shot down. Cade smacked Hooker on the shoulder, and the two exchanged glances. Clearly, I was missing something.

"Did the chief warn you I might drop by?"

"Don't he always?" Hooker cocked his head, narrowed his eyes. "Never cared before. Best not disrupt that pattern now."

Cade turned. "Sloane, I'd like you to meet one of my oldest friends, Quaid Hooker."

"Watch it with the 'old' insinuation. I'm the same age as you." Hooker stepped in front of me, drank me in. "You must be the infamous Sloane Monroe."

There it was. Again. Luckily the shock value had dulled to a manageable low. I'd come to expect it.

"Seems like everyone around here has heard of me," I said.

"You've been a topic of the chief's conversation a time or two."

The chief's and not Cade's this time. It should have been refreshing. But nothing the chief had to say about me ever was.

Hooker stifled a laugh. "Sorry to say when your name is mentioned, it usually has an expletive attached to it."

No sugar coating here.

"I suppose it's not easy for him to admit he wouldn't have solved the case he had last year without me," I said.

"You got it half right. This town saw you as the hero, not him. He probably figured he had plenty of time, and then all this retirement talk started."

"What you're saying is, I stole his legacy."

"Legacy or not, from what I know about you and your ability to solve every case you get, we needed you then and we need you now." Hooker swiveled, diverted his attention to Cade. "Shame we're meeting like this, man. I'm real sorry, for you and your family. Serena was one of the sweetest girls I've ever known."

"How did you know her?" I asked.

"Went to high school together. Always wanted to ask her out. Never got around to it though—not before Jack came along, snatched her up before I had the chance to reel her in for myself."

"Don't feel sorry for him," Cade teased. "He's never had a shortage of women in his life. Not then, not now."

"I'm a yellow," Hooker replied. "What do you expect?"

"A what?" I asked.

"Haven't you ever taken that personality test to see what color you are?"

I shook my head. "A yellow is … what?"

"Fun, outgoing, don't take life too seriously. Free-spirited. Charming, of course. Anyhow, some girl tested me. Said she was red so we couldn't be together, not that it mattered. I wasn't looking for a relationship at the time."

"At the time?" Cade joked. "I've never seen you in a relationship, not a lasting one."

"I dated Patrice for four months."

He said it like it was his crowning achievement. And I'd always thought *my* relationships were short.

"Four months is nothin' to brag about," Cade said.

Hooker smacked me on the shoulder, thumbed at Cade. "Just so you know, Cade here's a blue. At least in my opinion."

"And blues are …?"

"Don't change the subject by bringing it back to me," Cade said.

"Truth is," Hooker said. "I've never married."

"Some people never do," I said.

"I would, well, maybe I wouldn't marry. I'd entertain the idea of a relationship though, living together. It's just, I've never met a woman who could handle me enough to settle down."

I could think of one bright, beaming yellow who'd be up for the challenge: Miss Madison "Maddie" LaFoe.

"We can talk relationships later," Cade said. "Right now I need to know if there's anything you found during the autopsy that will give us any headway, help us locate Serena's killer."

"As far as bodies go, Serena's is clean. I didn't find any prints or fibers that didn't come from her house. No skin under the nails. No sign of a struggle. No sign of sexual assault. From what I can tell, the guy never touched her."

"What about the bullet wound?" Cade asked.

"The contact wound was consistent with the nature of her injury. As you probably know, she was shot once from behind, point-blank range, at a distance of just under three feet. The bullet, a forty-five caliber round, entered the back of her head, lodged in her skull. Whoever shot her got lucky."

"Why do you say that?" Cade asked.

"We're not talking about a heavy-duty gun here. Speaking of which, still no sign of the murder weapon?"

"Not to my knowledge." Cade ran a hand across his forehead. "Anything else?"

Hooker paused.

"What is it?" Cade asked.

"There is one other thing. Something I didn't expect to find. Serena had a slight amount of swelling in her lower abdomen."

"Do you know what caused it?"

"At first I wasn't sure. Once I opened her uterus, I saw something I didn't expect. A fetus."

"A what?"

"Are you saying Serena was pregnant?" I asked.

Hooker nodded.

"Around eleven weeks from what I can tell." Hooker looked at Cade. "I take it you didn't know?"

"I had no idea. Jack and Serena had been tryin' to conceive on their own for years. Serena was convinced she'd never be able to give birth on her own. That's why she adopted."

I wondered if Jack knew Serena was pregnant. If she, herself, knew she was pregnant. If anyone else knew, and whether it played a role in her murder if they did.

CHAPTER 21

Lime green Plymouth Barracudas weren't the variety of car people see every day. Standing inside of a run-down, yet immaculately clean auto body shop the next morning, I had to admit, even though the car didn't suit my taste, it looked like one hell of a sweet ride.

Cade knelt down, nudging a boy's pant leg with the tip of his boot. "Daniel Alvarez? We need to speak with you."

"The name's Danny," the boy shouted from beneath the Barracuda. "And I'm busy."

Cade yanked one of Danny's legs, ejecting Danny out from beneath the car. He squirmed, kicked at Cade's hand. Cade held tight, unwilling to relax his grip until the boy relented, smirked at Cade. "What's your problem, man? You deaf? I said I was busy."

Danny wasn't what I expected. With short, spiked, black hair and baggy, ripped jeans, he didn't look like the kind of guy a clean-cut Hannah would be attracted to—but what did I know about teenagers? Not much apparently.

"When's the last time you saw Hannah Kinkade?" Cade asked.

"What's it to you, bro?"

Cade reached out, his fingers twisting a knot into the front of Danny's shirt. "It's important, *bro*. Now answer the question."

"You her pops or somethin'? … cuz we're not together anymore."

Cade eased his jacket to the side with his free hand, flashed the badge clipped to the front of his jeans. "I'll ask again. When was the last time you saw her?"

"Two months ago maybe."

If what he said was true, it matched Renee's story of the birth father not being at the hospital when Hannah delivered Finn. It also meant he may have never seen his son before. Unless, of course, he was lying. There was always that. And I had to admit, Danny looked like a kid who'd had run-ins with the law before.

"I need details," Cade pressed.

"What *details?*"

"We need to know what happened the last time you saw Hannah," I said, "and what you know about the baby you two had together."

"I don't know a thing, mama. The two of you wasted your time comin' here, ahh–ight?"

It wasn't *ahh–ight* or all right. Not even close.

"We just want answers. Give them to us, and you can get back to your job."

Across the room, a rather oversized man with a thick, black mustache craned his neck to the side, peeking out the door of an office. His eyes were focused on Cade's hand wrung around Danny's shirt. A dollop of red sauce leaked from a foot-long meatball sub the man was holding, splotching onto the desk. The man unwound a piece of brown paper from a roll and half-wiped up the mess before setting the sandwich down on a stack of papers. His lack of sanitary measures bothered me to the point that I almost looked away.

The man stood and shuffled over, stopping once to shove his white, collared shirt inside his blue polyester pants. As soon as Danny saw Sandwich Guy en route, he performed a classic teenage eye roll and began speaking in rapid succession at Cade.

"I don't have to talk to you without a lawyer or somethin' like that, right? I mean, teck–nick–ally, you two can't do nothin' to me."

"What makes you think you need a lawyer?" Cade asked.

"Excuse me." Sandwich Guy looked at Cade's fisted hand then at Cade. "Who are you, and what's this about?"

"It doesn't concern you," Cade replied, his eyes never leaving Danny.

"I need you to take your hands off my son … or I'll call the police."

Danny's father seemed nice. Maybe *too* nice.

Danny sighed. "He *is* the police, Pop."

Cade removed his grip from Danny. Sandwich Guy stretched his hand out. I shook it. His grip was flaccid, weak.

"I'm Miguel Alvarez. And you are?"

"Sloane. And this is Cade. We're not trying to harass your boy. We just need to ask him a few questions."

"What kind of questions?"

"Mr. Alvarez, are you aware of your son's relationship with Hannah Kinkade?" I asked.

He nodded. "When they were together, my wife and I had Hannah over for dinner a few times."

"Stop talking," Danny cut in. "Why you gotta tell them stuff that isn't their business?"

"Danny, keep quiet. Let me handle this." Miguel looked at Cade. "I apologize for my son."

"Were you aware Hannah was pregnant?" Cade asked.

Father and son exchanged glances. Miguel *had* known about the baby. "I was. My wife was not."

"Why not tell your wife?"

"It would have been too hard on her if she knew Daniel and Hannah weren't keeping the boy. She would have wanted to raise the child herself. There would have been no talking her out of it. Not telling her was for the best."

On the far end of the shop, something clanked to the ground. It sounded like a wrench or a tool of some kind had slipped from one of the worker's hands. Miguel peered across the cars, lowered his voice. "Mind if we continue this conversation in my office?"

Cade and I followed Miguel to the back of the shop. Danny didn't move. He looked on as if he didn't feel it was necessary for him to be involved in the conversation now that his father was doing his dirty work for him. When Miguel discovered his son was no longer in tow, he swiftly rectified the situation. "Son, you too. Let's go."

With the door secured behind us, Miguel resumed our previous conversation. "I mean no disrespect, but why are you here asking questions? Daniel's child was adopted. We are trying to put it behind us, let him get on with his life."

"Mr. Alvarez," Cade asked. "Do you know about the newborn child that went missing earlier this week?"

"I watch the news. Why?"

"The baby that was kidnapped—his name is Finn. Finn is the child Hannah put up for adoption."

Danny slumped against the wall. He seemed numb, yet affected at the same time. The shock on his face looked real, as did Miguel's.

"Naw, naw, naw," Danny repeated. "I don't believe you. You're lying."

"I'm sorry, Danny," I said. "It's true. And now you know why we're here."

Danny turned away, clenched his hand, pulverized the drywall behind him. A chalk-like chunk crumbled apart, leaving a baseball-sized hole. Miguel seemed impervious to his son's actions. Instead of lashing out in anger, he put his hand on Danny's back, patted it a few times, his voice full of reassurance and concern. "I'm sorry, son."

"I have to ask you both," Cade said, "Where were you Monday night between the hours of midnight and six a.m.?"

"Home," Miguel said. "Sleeping, like everyone else."

"Can anyone verify this?"

"My wife, though as I stated before, she doesn't know about the baby. I'd like to keep it that way."

"I can't make any promises," Cade said. "If the chief wants to send someone to speak to your wife, your employees, or other members of your family, he will. Best you prepare yourself."

"I'm sure your wife would prefer to hear about it from you instead of the police," I added.

Danny remained against the wall, unmoving, giving no indication he was tuned in to the conversation.

"We're innocent," Miguel stated, "and we'd like to help you any way we can. What do you need to know?"

"Aside from the two of you, who else in your group of family and friends knew Hannah was pregnant?" Cade asked.

"No one."

"Is there any chance someone in your family found out about the baby, someone here, at your work?"

Miguel weaved his arms together, mulled over the question. "When Danny first came to me, told me about Hannah, we were alone in my pickup, driving on the highway. We discussed it two, maybe three more times, always just the two of us, always in the truck so we didn't risk anyone overhearing our conversation."

"Danny, is that true?" Cade asked.

"No one knows," Danny stammered. "Just us."

"We didn't want it to get out to our family," Miguel said. "Like I told you before, they would not have approved of the adoption."

"You said you saw Hannah a couple months ago, before she had the baby," Cade said. "Why did you see her? What did you talk about?"

"Hannah wanted to break up," Danny said. "I tried to talk her out of it."

"And did you?"

He shook his head.

"She said she didn't want to see me again. She said if I kept calling, she'd change her number."

"Why?"

His eyes bugged out. "I didn't want to keep the baby. Why you think?"

"Did you see her or talk to her after she ended the relationship?"

"I texted. She didn't respond. I went to her aunt's house. Her Aunt Ree's nice and all, but she never let me inside. She said Hannah couldn't see me yet. I never stopped tryin' though."

What had he meant by that? If she wouldn't take his calls and wouldn't see him, what else was there?

"When the baby was born, did anyone tell you?" I asked.

"Yeah. Her aunt sent me a picture of the kid before he left the hospital with his…whatever you call them."

"Adoptive parents?"

"Yeah. Those guys."

Miguel looked confused. Apparently he wasn't aware such a photo existed. Maybe not seeing his grandson was for the best. Then again, maybe seeing the baby motivated Danny to have a change of heart about giving up his son. Anything was possible.

"After seeing Finn, did you regret giving him up?" I asked.

"Naw. I felt better. I love Hannah. I'd do almost anything to be with her again, but I thought we were too young to raise a kid."

"You could have asked Hannah to abort the baby," I said. "I assume you didn't."

"Naw. My family don't believe in it."

"Choosing to give Finn life … it's a wonderful thing."

Danny curved his head toward me. "A wonderful thing? My kid is probably dead. Those people were supposed to protect him, take care of him, give him the kind of life I couldn't. They were supposed to keep him safe. They didn't. Hannah was right. I should have let her keep our son."

"It's not their fault Finn was taken."

"If we wouldn't have given him up, none of this would have happened. They looked like nice people. I don't get it."

How did he know what they looked like?

"You … saw them?" I asked. "When?"

Danny looked at his father, but it was far too late to fix his blunder.

"Danny, what do you mean they looked like nice people?" Miguel asked.

"I just mean … I only was trying to say …"

"Don't bother comin' up with some bullshit story to protect yourself," Cade said. "You've got one chance to be straight with me. If I don't believe you, if I think you're lyin', we'll take this conversation downtown."

"I followed them home," Danny said. "The people who adopted my kid."

"From where?"

"The hospital."

"Why?"

"I dunno. Curious, I guess. After Hannah's aunt sent me the picture, I went to the hospital, waited for them to come out. Figured they'd catch a plane, head out of town. Never thought they'd live so close by."

"So that's how Hannah knew where they lived."

"I wasn't ever gonna tell her. When she threatened never to speak to me again, I thought if I told her, it would fix things with us. Does she know our kid was nabbed?"

I nodded.

Danny looked at his father. "Hannah needs me, Dad. I gotta bounce."

"I'm afraid it isn't possible," I said.

"I don't care what you say, mama. I'm going whether you or your sidekick here like it or not."

"I'm not trying to keep you from her."

"What then?"

"Hannah's in the hospital. Her parents are there. They're not allowing anyone to see her or talk to her."

It was mostly true, and, given the way I was treated, I could only imagine how Aaron would react to meeting the boy who impregnated his daughter. For Hannah's sake, and for Daniel's, he needed to stay away. Far away.

Danny's nostrils flared. "She's in the hospital? Why?"

"Last night we went to see her," I said. "She didn't know about Finn. She hadn't been eating, and when her aunt told her the news, she collapsed. The news was more than she could handle."

"Oh, man. I gotta get out of here. I don't care what her parents want. I'm seeing her."

"No, son," Miguel said. "Give Hannah a day or two. Let her rest. Let her be with her family now."

"I can't, Pop. You don't get it. She can't be there. Alone. With *him*."

"With whom?" I asked. "What haven't you told your father, Danny?"

He shoved his hands in his pockets, refused to look at me. "Nothing. No one. Forget it."

"Danny, if you know something about Hannah's father, tell us. We can help her."

"I said nothing, and I'm not saying no more."

"Whatever you know, you're not helping her by remaining quiet."

"You don't get it," Danny said. "I'm done. Conversation over."

CHAPTER 22

I checked in with Renee by phone. She still hadn't seen Hannah, but she'd gained a momentary audience with Aaron. He agreed to return after he had dinner to talk things out. It didn't surprise me. Life seemed to revolve around his time frame, around the snap of his manipulative fingers.

Every day, every hour that ticked by, so did all hope of finding Finn. It seemed no matter where we turned, all we had was a bunch of leads that went nowhere. My brain wasn't pairing things together like it usually did. I was out of sorts, fuzzy, and I knew it. Cade knew it too. I could tell. He was counting on me. Finn was counting on me. They all were.

As strange as it seemed, we'd accepted an invitation to dine at Bonnie's house for dinner. Earlier she'd packed Jack's things and explained he'd be staying with her for an undetermined amount of time. It took a good deal of convincing before he warmed to the idea.

Not that he ever warmed. He wore down. Plain and simple. Bonnie insisted. She knew how desperately Jack needed family by his side before and after Serena's funeral. Maybe she was right, or maybe she was scared of what her son would do if he was left to his own devices again.

Part of me sided with Bonnie. For a moment I flashed back, remembering my own past, the crushing feeling of desperation I felt while standing inside my sister's home days after her death, looking one last time at the photos displayed on the wall, touching mementos she left behind. Even the faintest whiff of her balmy perfume percolating through an otherwise stale air had been toxic, not just to my heart, to my soul, and I knew I couldn't be there anymore. I couldn't go there again. To her house. With her memories. I had to get out, leave, and never return.

And I never did.

...

Before dinner, we headed back to Cade's house to pick up Shelby. The turnoff to his one-lane dirt road was blocked by an idling SUV belonging to the police department. A man stood outside the vehicle, his back braced against the driver's-side door. When Cade's truck came into the man's line of sight, the man rocked his body forward, slapped a stubborn dirt stain off his pants, overlapped one arm over the other. Waited.

Cade pulled to the side. The truck lulled to a stop. Cade didn't get out. He lowered the window, stared at Chief Rollins like he'd expected him to show up sooner or later. Too bad it wasn't later.

"Chief."

"McCoy."

"Anything new on my cousin's case?"

"I could ask you the same question," the chief said. "I hear you two have had a very active day, or should I say *days*."

"How's that?"

"Don't play dumb with me, McCoy. I know all about where you and little-miss-know-it-all have been. There've been sightings of the two of you all around town."

Cade sighed. "No need to waste your breath on another lecture. I'm not interested."

"Don't disrespect me, McCoy. I ordered you off this case, though you don't seem to give a damn."

"I'm well aware of what you said."

"And … what?" the chief questioned. "You think you're above it all now? Nothing I say means anything to you?"

"I never said—"

"I want you to leave."

The chief wasn't looking at Cade anymore. He was looking at me.

"Tonight, tomorrow morning, whatever," he continued. "As long as you're gone. You must be proud of yourself, thinkin' you had me convinced you weren't takin' cases no more."

He paused like he expected me to spout off, overreact. I didn't. Why would I? What difference would it have made if I had?

"She's not goin' anywhere," Cade said. "If you want someone to blame, blame me. I asked for her help."

The chief shifted his focus to Cade. "As for you, I've made some calls. Don't think because of the relationship I had with your father, or because you're hopin' to assume my position, that you're at liberty to do whatever you like."

Hoping to assume ... interesting choice of words, spoken like he had the power of veto, like he could wave his gun-slinging wand in the air and Cade's newly-appointed job would be dissolved, off the table, like it had never been there in the first place. The offer had been extended and accepted, so I was either missing something, or the chief had resorted to throwing a senior-citizen-sized tantrum in the hopes Cade could be swayed. My gut said it was the latter.

As Cade formed a response, Chief Rollins raised himself back onto the seat of his SUV, letting him know he was unwilling to hear it. The door closed. The chief didn't look back. He didn't utter another word. He'd said what he came to say. Tantrum over. He mounted a wrist over the top of a worn, leather steering wheel and pressed on the gas. I turned, watching the dust coat the air in a thin, foggy haze.

"I won't stand in the way of your job," I said to Cade. "You're not losing it. Not because of me."

Cade put the truck back into gear and pulled onto the road again. "There's nothin' he can do, Sloane. Nothin'. Trust me."

"Did you hear what he said? He dangled your upcoming position over your head. Sounded like a threat to me."

"He's just blowin' off steam. The job's mine. Even if it weren't, it wouldn't matter. I'd do what I'm doin' even if you decided to leave." He glanced at me, a look of concern in his eyes. "You haven't thought of leavin', have you?"

"And miss out on the opportunity of a personal, police escort out of town?" I smiled. "Not a chance."

There was a certain kind of satisfaction that came with defying a person I didn't particularly like. A satisfaction begging to be uncorked. Stirring the pot,

168 C h e r y l   B r a d s h a w

pushing buttons. It was in my grandfather's blood. It was in mine.

From a distance, an outline of a female I assumed was Shelby came into view. She was running, sprinting toward Cade's truck at full speed, the expression on her face a mixture of bewilderment, fury.

Something wasn't right.

I speculated about the kind of trouble she'd gotten herself into this time.

Cade's foot hammered down on the brake, the truck skidding to a stop. He stared into the distance, his eyes darting from Shelby to a second woman following close behind. He leaned forward to get a better look, his pupils expanding twice their size when reality reached out and struck him in the face. Wendy. Back for round two. Two inaudible dings rang inside my head.

Tears streamed down Shelby's face as she saw her safe place, the one person who'd never let her down a day in her life, no matter how much she pressed, how much she pushed him. "Dad!"

Cade exited the truck, his arms outstretched. "I know. I'm sorry. I should have told you. I was going to tell you."

"You knew she was here and you didn't say anything? Why, Dad? How could you?"

"Shelby, please. Wait. I just wanna talk to you." Wendy rested her hands on her knees, panting, short of breath. "If you would just let me explain."

"No!" Shelby retorted. "I don't want you here."

"I'm your mother, honey. And I always will be whether you choose to stay mad at me or not."

With her father there to provide support, Shelby found her courage again. She pivoted, broke from her father's embrace, faced Wendy. "Don't call yourself that. Don't call yourself my mother. You're *not* my mother. Mother's don't abandon their children just because life gets in the way sometimes. I don't want you, and *I* ... don't ... need ... you."

"You're angry. You need time to let it all sink in. Maybe in a day or two when you've calmed down, I'll come back, and we can talk. Things will be different this time. You'll see."

"You're not comin' back," Cade clarified.

"I told you, Cade, I'm not going anywhere. I'm staying."

"You're not welcome here. If you stay, you won't be well received. Not be me. Not by anyone."

"*Well received?*" Wendy tossed her head back, snickered. "Who have you been hanging around that has you acting all refined?"

"Time for you to go, Wendy."

"I came to see my daughter. You can't stop me. You can't shut me out like this. No matter what's happened, we're family."

"You're *not* my family," Shelby seethed. "I hate you!"

Wendy's hand whipped back then sprung forward just like I anticipated it would. I caught her wrist between my fingers, a few inches before it collided with its target—Shelby's face. I could have stopped there, been the better person, given Wendy her hand back. I'd already stopped her from harming her daughter. But I wasn't in a forgiving kind of mood. I was in a lesson-teaching kind.

I positioned my body in front of Wendy, shielded her from Shelby so there wasn't a chance of Shelby being attacked again. I used my pointer finger to press down, apply pressure to the center of the back of Wendy's hand, bending it forward just enough for her to whimper in pain. I curved my face toward hers, my voice low. "Cade's a gentleman. He won't hurt you because you're a woman. Even if he wanted to, he wouldn't because his mother raised him right. My mother raised me not to tolerate people like you. If you ever lay a hand on Shelby again, I'm going to show you just how intolerant I can be. Understand?"

I bent her hand a bit more just in case she didn't. She looked like she wanted to cry. Point made. I let go.

Wendy flicked her hand in the air like she was trying to breathe life back into it. "You're a bitch."

I grinned. "I know."

It wasn't the worst thing I'd been called.

Wendy looked at Cade. "She assaulted me! Are you just gonna stand there, let her get away with it?"

Interesting statement considering she'd just tried to strike her child.

"I didn't see anything," Shelby sneered. "How 'bout you, Dad?"

Cade shrugged.

"The only thing I saw was you attempt to physically assault my daughter." He dangled a pair of cuffs in the air.

"You're arresting me?! Now wait a minute, Cade. Think this through. Don't do this."

"Oh, I have thought about it."

"All right, all right. I'll leave. Just … don't arrest me. I'm kinda on … I just can't be …"

"Kinda on what?"

She turned, stared into nothing. "Two years' probation."

"What's that supposed to mean?" Cade asked. "Probation for what?"

"Bar fight. It wasn't my fault. I swear."

"I bet it never is," I said.

"Look—the whore came at me," Wendy said. "I was just defending myself."

"And yet, you still received two years," I added.

"Don't act like you know what went on. You don't."

I could see where this was going, see Wendy making the same kind of commitment to Cade that she never lived up to in the past. Girl makes boy promise to leave, boy uses the last shred of faith he has in the girl, believes she might actually mean what she says this time, do what he asks. Okay, so maybe I'd let my mind run rampant. Fact was, I didn't know Wendy. I didn't need to—I knew her type. And I wasn't going to watch her destroy him again.

"I'll give Wendy a personal escort back to wherever it is she's staying," I offered.

"I'll do it," Cade said. "It should be me."

"Your cousin needs you. Go spend time with him."

Wendy was less than thrilled with the idea. "My car is here. Neither of you need to—"

"I'm here to make sure you leave," I said.

"I meant after the funeral," Wendy said. "Not before."

"Let me ask you this," I said. "When's the last time you talked to Serena, because no one seems to know the two of you stayed in contact. Serena never mentioned that fact to Cade. Not once."

She hesitated. "I asked her not to mention it. I didn't want him to know where I was living. Thought it was better that way, for everyone."

"Wendy, it's best if you don't come to the funeral," Cade said.

"Cade, I came here because—"

"You're not to attend the funeral."

"Let's go," I said.

"Like I said. My car's here. I don't need a ride."

"I don't care. You're getting one. I'll bring you back to your car once you're packed."

And then I'd watch her leave.

CHAPTER 23

The drive to Wendy's hotel involved a fair amount of crickets for the first few minutes, a blissful blend of calm and reflective quiet. Fine by me. I had no desire to kick-start her shrill, nasally tone again. Too bad the silence didn't last.

"You're his girlfriend, aren't you?" Wendy asked.

The woman was like a parrot with a one-track mind.

"If by girlfriend you're asking if I'm a girl and Cade's friend, then yes. I am."

She half laughed, half looked like she wanted to bulldoze the snarky grin I'm sure I wore on my face. I didn't blame her. If the roles were reversed, I'd probably feel the same.

"You always such a smart ass?"

I considered the accusation. Guilty as charged.

"You can't have him," she blurted.

"Cade's not a piece of property. He can decide for himself what he wants."

"I take it you think what he wants is you?"

There was that shrill, nasally tone again.

She unzipped her red, pleather bag and pulled out a cigarette and a lighter. I pinched the cigarette in between my fingers, chucked it in the backseat. "You're not lighting up in my car."

"I need one. Bad."

"I don't care."

She brought her knees to her chest, leaned back, sulked like she was in grade school.

"Did you really come here to rekindle your relationship?" I asked. "I mean, so far it's not working out. Why not tell the truth?"

"What *truth?*"

"Why are you really here?"

"I never stopped loving him, you know."

I got the impression her idea of love was far different than mine.

"And you think he returns your feelings?"

"When I first saw him again, I convinced myself it was possible. He's bullheaded. Always has been. I knew he'd resist at first. I guess I thought if I hung around, gave him time, I could find a way to bring him back to me."

"You say it like you're not sure you believe it anymore."

"I saw the way he looked at you. He used to look at me that way too."

I felt sticky, like my bra had fused to my skin. I fought the urge to open the window, lean out, fan myself. I knew Cade didn't love her, not like he once had. Whether or not the two of us were friends or building something more, that one truth should have pacified me. Instead, I felt bothered, anxious to get her out of town.

Wendy pushed her legs back down, winced.

"What's wrong with you?" I asked.

"Nothing."

It wasn't nothing—it was something. She was in pain, and I couldn't imagine her short trek up Cade's dirt road was the culprit. I peeled back the edge of her shirt with a finger, stared at the exposed discoloration beneath.

She jerked to the side, yanked her shirt back down. "Don't touch me!"

My three-second glimpse allowed me to view a sizable bruise, about the size of my hand, beneath her right breast. Given the lack of clothing she wore, I didn't know how I'd missed it. As bruises go, fresh bruises were red, older ones changed from green to a yellowish-brown as they reached the end of the healing process. Wendy's bruise was purplish-blue in color, which meant it was somewhere between two and five days old.

"Where did you get it?" I asked.

"Nowhere."

"Lie about it if you want. You lie about everything else."

"Why do you care?"

I didn't.

"I don't want whoever you're running from showing up here," I said. "I don't want Cade involved in the mess you call a life. We have a baby to find. He doesn't have time to fight your battles for you."

"I haven't asked for his help. Even if I needed it, I still wouldn't."

The question was—why?

I parked the car in front of a desolate, rundown hotel I'd always assumed had been abandoned. Maybe it was, or maybe she'd broken in and was staying for free. With its broken windows and weather-worn doors with chipped, orange paint, I wouldn't have been shocked to learn the place had been condemned.

"Get your stuff," I said. "I'll wait here."

I reclined the seat back a few notches, just enough to keep my eye on the unbalanced prize while maintaining a comfortable position. Wendy entered the hotel room, left the door ajar, turned on the light. Since there was only one way out, through the front, she had nowhere else to go but back out the same door again.

The first few minutes passed without incident. Around the four-minute mark, I heard what sounded like objects being tossed around. She obviously had a temper, but this was ridiculous.

Sit tight. Let her get all the angst out of her system. She won't be your problem much longer.

Except she *was* my problem now, a throbbing, tenacious pain in my ass, and in the last minute, that pain had gone from quiet to raging lunatic back to quiet again. I had a sickening feeling my assumptions about her hissy fit had been wrong.

I pawed beneath my seat, retrieved my gun, crept over to Wendy's door, and peeked through the slit. She wasn't alone. Kneeling over her limp body was a man, his plumber's crack on full display. His knees pressed into the springs of the cheap, thin mattress. The man's melon-sized hands wrapped around Wendy's neck, exerting pressure. Her eyes were closed, unresponsive. From my vantage point, I couldn't tell whether she was alive or dead. She wasn't moving.

There was no time to negotiate or argue. It was obvious he intended to take Wendy's life. I fired a single shot. It connected, striking him in the forearm, like I'd intended. He released Wendy, howling as he clamped a hand down on his arm.

The man examined me like, even though I'd caught him committing murder, of the two of us, *I* was the crazy one. Without removing my finger from the trigger, I used my other hand to dial 911. I spat the address to the person who answered. Once they confirmed, I hung up, shifted my attention back to the man.

"Touch her again and the next bullet kills you," I said.

"Wendy's druggie friend, come to save the day with her toy gun."

His knowledge of guns and non-drug addicts was obviously limited.

"Hands up. Get up. Back against the wall. Now!"

"Which is it," he joked. "Get up, hands up, or back away?"

"All three. Move it!"

He stood, remaining at the side of the bed, shielding me from Wendy's view. I needed to know if she was alive. And I needed to know now. I popped off another shot, this time narrowly missing his crotch. Message received. We had movement.

"Keep going until you're against the wall," I said.

"There's two. How many bullets you have left in that gun?"

"Enough to kill *you*."

I made my way over to Wendy, applied two fingers to the side of her neck. Her pulse was faint, her breathing shallow, but it was there. Unsure of whether or not she'd suffered a spinal injury after the beating she'd just taken, I couldn't jeopardize causing additional injuries by moving her. In the meantime, I had one more call to make. I just didn't want to make it.

"Move and you die," I said as I dialed the number.

The greeting I received when the call was answered was just what I expected. "You gone yet, Monroe? Because if you aren't—"

"Shut up and listen," I said. "Someone just tried to kill Cade's ex-wife."

"Disrespect aside, explain to me why I'm supposed to care?"

"Because Wendy's here in Jackson Hole, which means the attempted murder happened in *your* town. Call Cade, let him know, and then get to the Wildflower Motel."

I shoved the phone inside my pocket. No more distractions.

"You planning on letting me stand here until I bleed to death?" the man asked.

One could only hope.

"Makes no difference to me whether you live or die. You attempted to take Wendy's life. You may have even succeeded. You don't deserve my help."

"I have to say, this is unexpected. I didn't think the whore had a friend in the world."

She probably didn't.

"Didn't think anyone would miss her if she was gone either," he continued.

"Who are you to her anyway? Her dealer? Does she owe you money?"

He roared with laughter. "That's rich. The whore's my wife. Cheated on me. Caught her in bed with the guy. Friend of mine. Well … ex-friend as of late."

Sirens echoed outside.

Hang on, Wendy. Hang on.

"You try and kill him too, your ex-friend?"

The way he eyeballed me turned my stomach. "Wouldn't you like to know?"

"Wendy cheated, and you thought you'd beat her, teach her a lesson. Until she ran. Bet you didn't predict that."

"No one runs from me. *No one.*"

I stepped aside as local officers blew through the door.

"You can put the gun down, Monroe."

The chief walked in with two additional officers by his side. In a way, I was relieved to see him. In another, I prepped myself for what might come next. He brushed past me, ignored me like I wasn't there. Medics followed, immediately going to work on Wendy.

"Dean Sanders," the chief said to the man against the wall. "I hear everyone's lookin' for you."

Dean shrugged. "You found me. You want a prize?"

"Oh, I believe you in police custody is prize enough," the chief said. "You're a wanted man in Cheyenne."

Wendy sucked in a breath and gasped. Her eyes burst open. She seemed disoriented, unfamiliar with her current surroundings.

"How is she?" the chief asked.

A young female with her hair in a long, brown ponytail said, "Weak. We need to get her to the hospital."

"Keep me informed."

Dean was cuffed, taken outside, and shoved with a great deal of force into the back of a squad car. I stood, watched the glow from the ambulance's flashing lights disappear down the road.

Chief Rollins turned his attention to me. "We'll need to get a statement. You waitin' on McCoy?"

I nodded.

"I'd like to talk to him first. Is that all right?" I asked.

"Are you actually askin' me for permission?"

"I am."

"I don't know how you do it."

"Do what?" I asked.

"Always end up in the wrong place at the right time."

"Dean would have killed her if I didn't—"

"Save it. Wendy's boyfriend's dead. A couple hunters found his body on a mountain a few days ago. He'd been shot a half a dozen times. You did the right thing here. I'm sure you didn't want to call me. Good thing you did."

"Dean said he caught her cheating on him."

"That's what he called it? From what I was told, she'd tried to divorce Dean several times before. When he wouldn't grant the divorce, she tried to move on with her life the only way she knew how."

The situation reminded me of a quote I once read about judging a person without knowing what they were going through. I found myself seeing Wendy in a new, yet even more complicated light. While I was skeptical about her true desire to get her family back, I'd critiqued her harshly. Too harshly. She was desperate, seeking sanctuary, and all I'd done was do everything in my power to send her on her way.

Cade arrived with Shelby, both hopping out of the truck as soon as it came to a stop.

"She's already gone," I said. "The ambulance just left."

"What happened?"

I filled him in on the details. "I think she found out her boyfriend was dead and she panicked, realized it was possible she was next. She came here because she didn't have anywhere else to go."

"Why didn't she just say that then?" Cade asked. "Instead of messin' with us like she did? If I knew she was in trouble, bad feelin's aside, I would have helped her."

"Those are questions you'll have to ask Wendy yourself. She's on her way to the hospital now. You should go."

"I … I don't know."

"She doesn't have anyone, Cade."

Shelby entwined her arm inside her father's. "We could stop by, Dad. Just see how she's doing. We don't have to stay long."

Cade picked up on Shelby's change of heart, realizing what he needed to do—if not for Wendy—for his daughter.

"I'll call Bonnie," he said. "Tell her what happened, let her know we'll stop by tomorrow. You're welcome to come with us."

I shook my head.

"You two go ahead. I'll meet you back at the house later."

Shelby's noodly arms wound around my body, embracing me. "Thank you, Sloane. Thank you for saving her. I love you."

She loves me.

I could have taken it for what it was—a comment uttered during an intense moment—except she looked me in the eye when she said it. I could see the sincerity, the palpable emotion.

"I … love you too," I said.

The words, so short, so simple, rolled off my tongue like I was having difficulty communicating in a foreign language. How long had it been since I'd uttered them?

Far too long.

CHAPTER 24

Somehow I knew when the day first started it was going to be a long one. After I told my side of things to a couple of overeager cops, I left, managing to get two or three breaths in before my phone buzzed. Renee. Telling me Hannah was gone. Gone how, exactly, I wasn't sure yet. Renee was unhinged, incapable of complete, rational sentences.

Once I was able to bring Renee's heightened sensitivity down to a manageable level, the story was clear. Renee had never met with Hannah's dad, Aaron, after dinner. The meeting, or the promise to meet, had been a diversion, a way to pacify Renee while Aaron removed Hannah from the hospital. Quietly. Under the radar.

There was little to be done. Although Hannah was of legal age, she'd agreed to leave with her parents. She even signed the paperwork to check herself out. Renee had called Hannah and Aaron dozens of times. No one answered.

My unrelenting instinct to rush to Hannah's aid and save her from her oppressive father had me fighting with myself about whether to get involved. Sure, Aaron was a threat, a man to be taken seriously. But even if I did rescue Hannah, who was to say she wouldn't go back to him again? She wasn't my daughter. Wasn't my responsibility. Wasn't my case. If there was one lesson my grandmother taught me when she took me away, it was that I needed to find a way to start letting things go. No matter how hard I tried, I couldn't save everyone from their own worst enemy—themselves.

I promised Renee I'd remain close to my phone. I reminded her that Hannah was old enough to make her own decisions. We needed to trust her, give her wings, let her learn how to fly on her own.

It was a quarter to ten. Cade and Shelby weren't back from the hospital yet. I tried not to think about it, as if that was possible. I was in desperate need of a diversion.

My grandfather's journal was tucked away in a zippered compartment in my suitcase. Every night before bed I told myself I was going to open it, read a page, or two, or five, learn things about him I didn't know before, learn things about myself. Of my short list of relatives, we were alike in the kind of way people referred to as "uncanny," although I never liked that word much. It was on *my* short list of words I abhorred, along with terms like "chuckled" and "moist," two words that made me cringe every time I heard them.

I flipped the first page of the journal open, read the date. 1957. Before he joined the FBI. It seemed like a lifetime ago. It was. Beneath the entry was a name. Celia Wilcox. Whoever she was, she'd been missing. Two weeks and they hadn't found her. The last time she was seen she had been with her boyfriend, Clifford Sweeney. After interviewing him, checking his alibi, my grandfather believed he was innocent. I was in the middle of turning the next page when my phone rang. Again. And again it was Renee.

"She texted me," Renee said.

"Hannah?"

"Yes. Only, the text came from Ann's phone, not Hannah's."

Strange.

"What did the text say?"

"It's Hannah. Help me."

"Did you respond? Did you call her?"

"Of course, I did. I've called ten times in the last five minutes. She's not answering. I'm leaving. I'm going to her house. I don't care what Aaron thinks. I don't care what anyone thinks. She's my niece."

I thought about cautioning her to wait until we could verify what was going on first. It wouldn't have mattered. I closed my grandfather's journal, slipped it back inside my bag, and said, "Wait. I'm coming with you."

CHAPTER 25

Cade still hadn't returned when Renee arrived to get me. It seemed odd he'd stay at the hospital so long, but then, everything seemed odd lately, off course, like a misguided ship on a blackened night. I thought about calling him. I *wanted* to call him, if for nothing more than to soothe my curious nerves, my insecurities about the odds that he'd seen Wendy in a different light. She'd survived an almost successful attempt on her life. It was enough to melt the most jaded, unforgiving heart. Was it enough to melt his? If he *had* softened toward her, I'd detect it in his voice, and I couldn't bear it. Not now.

I grabbed a pen that had been erroneously placed inside a basket of nearly-spoiled apples and rifled through one drawer, then another, looking for anything suitable to write on. I settled for the back of an unopened bill.

Gone with Renee to check on Hannah.
Explain more later.

Be back soon.

Don't wait up.

–Sloane

Ever since Wendy dropped back into Cade's life, I'd felt something more for him, *feelings* maybe. At first I chalked it up to my insatiable need to play the role of protector. Now I wasn't sure I'd properly diagnosed my feelings. Was it possible I'd mistaken feelings of love with feelings of jealousy?

. . .

The drive from Jackson Hole to Hannah's parents' house in Idaho Falls was almost two hours each way. Renee was too preoccupied with thoughts of why Hannah had sent the text to engage in any kind of meaningful conversation. This was fine by me. It gave me time to process, time to wonder about things like whether Hannah herself had sent the message for help from her mother's phone because Aaron had taken her phone away, or if her mother had sent it on Hannah's behalf. Most people wouldn't even question it. They'd just accept what was presented to them as fact. People were predictable that way, always focusing on one side of a coin instead of flipping it over, factoring in all the possibilities. Life was easier seeing things for what they appeared to be, instead of pushing past the smoke to get to the mirror, the truth.

It reminded me of a Christmas card. The kind with the boisterous, beaming family on the front, and a yearly "what we've been up to" letter on the inside. At first glance, the family really seemed perfect. So perfect, in fact, the recipients of the card might even find themselves dwelling on their own bundle of shortcomings just looking at the photo of the family and the excellent smiles plastered on all of their faces. If only they looked behind the flashy grins, the accolades of praise and unrealistic perfection, they'd see the cracks. Or maybe they didn't look, and instead, accepted a life blinded by reality. Next year, when that same family seemed to be falling apart, they would say they never saw it coming. They probably didn't. Their eyes weren't open.

Mine were.

The way I saw it, Ann could have sent the text just as easily as Hannah could have. She seemed like the type of person who would go to extreme measures in order to avoid any blame berthing on her own shoulders. I imagined a time long before Aaron came around, a time when Ann was her own person, confident and unwavering. Through the years I assumed Aaron had picked her apart, day by day, whittling Ann's armor down to nothing. He'd destroyed the woman she used to be and created a new one, one suited just for him, a Stepford wife.

Marriage wasn't supposed to be that way. It was meant to bond two people together, not break them apart. In my experience, relationships didn't just break apart, they shattered. I wanted to believe in marriage, the fairy tale, the knight in shining armor trotting into my life atop a glorious, white horse. The truth was, I no longer believed in marriage, and I hadn't for a long time.

I thought about Aaron, and a far more sinister scheme came to mind: What if *he* had sent the message to Renee in a devious effort to lure her to the one place he maintained control? Hashing things out in the privacy of his home would shield him from his harshest critic, the public eye, keeping him and his fits of rage safe. As unnerving as it was, I actually preferred this theory to the others. Because if Aaron hadn't sent the text, odds were Hannah was in grave danger.

Thirty minutes outside of Idaho Falls, my phone lit up. Cade.

"Where are you?" he asked.

"Did you get my note?"

"Yeah. Why didn't you call me? I would have gone with you."

"I didn't know how long you were going to be with Wendy. I didn't feel right bothering you."

"You're not a bother, Sloane, and you never could be."

"I thought maybe the two of you needed time to talk things out."

"Now hold on. Are you sayin' you didn't get my text message?"

I hadn't, although I wasn't surprised. "My service has been weird up here. I don't think I'm getting my messages. Not all of them, anyway. What did it say?"

"I only spent about fifteen minutes with Wendy. Spent the rest of the time over at my aunt's house with Jack."

I couldn't deny it—I was relieved. "How is he?"

"About the same," Cade said. "Had a chance to talk to him one-on-one for a bit. I told him I'd seen Hooker, and he asked if I knew."

"About Serena's pregnancy?"

"Yeah."

"So he was aware she was pregnant."

"Guess they were plannin' on makin' a big deal about it. Had an idea cooked up about gettin' everyone together, havin' Finn wear a shirt sayin' he was gonna be a big brother."

My stomach lurched just hearing about their plans. In less than a week, Jack had lost his wife, his son, his unborn child. Everything, taken in an instant.

"He asked me not to tell anyone about the baby for now," Cade continued. "Said the only one they'd mentioned it to was Grace."

"I'm sorry I couldn't be there … with you … with him."

"Don't be. You gonna tell me what you're doin' though?"

Realizing he might think I was crazy for chasing after something I hoped would lead to nothing more than a misinterpretation, I filled him in.

"I need to know she's all right," I said when I finished. "For my own peace of mind. Maybe it's selfish, but I won't feel—"

"I understand."

He understood.

No explanation needed.

"Do what you need to do," he said. "I'm here if you need me. Until then, I think I'll stay up for a while."

"You don't need to worry about me. I'll be fine."

"I'll see you when you get here."

It was his way of saying he was staying up regardless of anything I said to try to sway him. I saw no reason to fight it. I respected his strong, stubborn attitude. I identified with it as well. Too well.

We said our goodbyes as Renee turned down Hannah's street. Street lamps paved the way to an otherwise dark, two-story house. I glanced at the time. Just past midnight. The soft night air offered an illusion that all was calm, quiet. It seemed to say there was nothing to see here, nothing to fear. I hoped it was true.

We parked along the curb in front of a mature oak tree. Renee unbuckled her seatbelt, curled her fingers around the door latch. I yanked on her arm, stopping her.

"What?" she asked. "I've been waiting over two hours for this moment. We need to get in there. Now."

"Let's be smart about it. We have no idea how Aaron will react when he sees you here. Part of me thinks Aaron set all of this up on purpose."

"You think *he* texted me?"

"It's possible. Maybe he wanted to get you alone."

"No. Hannah sent it. I feel it in my gut."

It didn't matter what I said. She'd never see past the smoke.

"If he refuses to allow you to see Hannah," I said, "we will have come all this way for nothing."

She sighed. "All right, fine. I'll do it your way. I'll try to, at least. What do you suggest?"

"Where's Hannah's room?"

Renee pointed to a window on the far right side of the house. "Hannah's on the main level. Aaron and Ann's room is upstairs on the opposite end."

We'd caught our first lucky break. Hopefully we could turn one into two.

"I'm going to get out first and make my way to Hannah's room," I said. "Wait until I'm there. I'll signal you. That's your cue to go to the front door. We both know Aaron will answer. When he does, I don't want you to blow up. You must remain calm."

"I can't promise—"

"Do you want to make sure Hannah's all right or not?"

She nodded.

"Then we need to be smart," I said. "I'm counting on you to buy me some time. Give me the chance to get into Hannah's room without him thinking anything is amiss. Pace yourself, don't rush. I'll need as much time as you can get me."

"I don't know how to keep him there. What am I supposed to say?"

"Play to his larger-than-life self-admiration. Tell him you drove here because you want to make things right. Apologize if you have to for everything that's happened. Tell him you know you made a mistake.

Promise you'll never do it again. Make him feel like all of his opinions are right, and you're the one that's wrong."

"I'm not sorry."

I was starting to doubt her capabilities. "You're missing the point, Renee. There's a time to be honest, and there's a time to lie. Stroke his ego. It seems to be the only thing he responds to, so just this once, use it to your advantage. Whatever happens, you need to sell it. He *must* believe you. Can you do it?"

"I think so."

"I don't need you to think," I said. "I need you to know. Just be careful, okay?"

"How will I know when to stop?"

"When you see me, you can drop the charade. By then we'll have the answers we need. Got it?"

She pressed her hands to her jeans like she was preparing for the biggest role of her life. I just hoped she could pull it off. Either way, we were about to find out.

CHAPTER 26

With the gentlest of movements, I eased the car door open, exited the car, and crouched down, watching, waiting to see if any lights illuminated upstairs. Thirty seconds later, there was no change. I crossed the lawn, my focus shifting to Renee. Her face was stony, frenetic. Ready for a fight. Faking her anger wouldn't be easy, and I was teetering on the fence of whether she'd be successful or not.

I reached the edge of the house, stood in front of Hannah's window, turned back, gave Renee the green light. She exited the car, closing the door like she would on any other day, not realizing the reverberation alone was enough to rouse the street from its restful slumber.

I reached Hannah's darkened room, assessed her window. It was garden-variety, no frills, with a slide-release latch. I pressed both hands against the glass and attempted to lift up. It was locked.

Renee approached the front steps of the house. She paused briefly, ingesting a deep breath before climbing a series of stairs, removing her from my line of sight. I cupped my hands on both sides of my face and peered through Hannah's window.

A dull, almost burned-out nightlight plugged into an outlet next to the bed did nothing to enhance my vision. I slid a hand inside my pocket, pulled out a set of keys dangling from a small flashlight key chain. I clicked the flashlight on, beaming circular light through the window. I hoped Hannah wouldn't see the glow from my light and feel compelled to scream.

Hannah's bed was unmade and empty, with one exception—a pillow-sized stuffed bunny or bear was positioned haphazardly on its side. A polka-dot comforter was crumpled into a pile in the middle, like Hannah had gone to bed earlier, then got back up again. I considered the various options. Maybe she was in the bathroom or grabbing a late-night snack. Or maybe, if she'd sent the message to Renee, she'd heard us drive up and started for the front door.

The sound of Aaron's dictatorial voice filled the air with a blitz of one-sided attacks aimed at Renee. I couldn't make out all the verbal garbage, but I understood a few. "You've got some nerve coming here." And then, "You've no right—this isn't your business."

The fragmented sentences fanned across the yard, piercing the silence. His nervous apprehension told me one thing: Aaron was genuinely shocked to see her there. He hadn't sent the message.

My plan to distract him had worked, so far. Now I needed to find Hannah. If the latch on her window hadn't been locked, I would have assumed she snuck out at some point after her parents retired to bed for the evening. She'd contemplated running away before. It was plausible she'd built up enough pent-up rage to go through with it this time.

While I pondered my next plan of attack, which involved finding another window to crawl through, Aaron's voice abruptly died out. Either Renee had been successful at calming her brother down, or he'd slammed the door in her face, denying entry. I arched my head just enough to see the porch had been deserted. She'd made it inside.

I returned to an upright position, my flashlight catching a glimpse of something that, at first glance, appeared to be nothing more than an article of clothing on the floor next to the bed. On second glance, I saw something else—two feet sticking out from what I now believed to be a pair of flannel pajamas.

I repositioned the flashlight, stuck my face against the glass, looked again.

It couldn't be.

But it was.

Hannah.

I could see the bottom half of her body. Nothing else. The rest of her was concealed by the bed. A numbing sensation rushed through me, my mind filtering through various scenarios about why she'd collapsed to the floor, for a second time. I needed to get to her. Fast.

The window to the right of Hannah's room was locked and too small for my body to fit through even if it had been open. I was desperate and short on time. I tried the next one over, deciding if I failed again, I'd return to Hannah's window, shattering the damn thing if it meant getting inside.

The latch on the third window was bent just enough to render it closed, but not locked enough to keep me out. I removed the window screen and took a chance I could get it open. The window was jammed, unwilling to open at first. I braced one foot against the side of the house and pulled with everything I had. Success. The window rolled open. I clicked off the flashlight and climbed inside a vacant spare bedroom that was set up for sewing, ironing, and laundry. I eased my way into the hall. Heard voices. Aaron was talking, in full lecture mode. Renee was crying. Impressive. I heard nothing from Ann, but then, I hadn't ever heard anything from Ann.

Keep up the charade, Renee. Just a little longer.

I slinked inside Hannah's room, closed the door, locked it. I flipped on the bedroom light, hoping with the door closed, I wouldn't draw attention to myself. Hannah's eyes were closed. If she *had* fainted again, she was out cold, her body stationary. While I knelt down, reached out to her, my eyes darted around the room, bouncing from one item to another, taking it all in at once. An empty prescription bottle on its side on Hannah's nightstand, an ultrasound photo clutched in her hand, a phone on the dresser that wasn't hers, a ripped piece of notebook paper on the floor, in between the bed and the nightstand.

"No … no … no … Hannah, please," I begged. "Please Hannah, can you hear me?"

Nothing.

I wanted to slap her, anything to evoke a response. I positioned my cheek next to her mouth, stared down at her chest. Watched. Waited. Nothing. No breath. Hands trembling, I jabbed at the speaker button on my phone, somehow managing to quell my trembling hands long enough to call for help.

I placed the heel of my hand on Hannah's chest, rested the other hand on top, fingers interlocked. While

I attempted to "stay calm" as the woman on the phone instructed, like it was truly possible in a screwed-up situation like this, I started chest compressions.

My conversation with the woman on the other end of the line gave me away, like I knew it would. I no longer cared. Let Aaron come. Let them all come. And they did. A parade of footsteps scampered toward Hannah's room, heavy and fast, on a mission. I couldn't allow them to bother me. Hannah was all that mattered now.

I pinched Hannah's nose closed, secured my lips over her mouth, blew inside, wishing something, anything would make a difference, even though nothing did. The door handle jiggled.

"Why in the hell is this locked?" Aaron yelled. "Hannah, open this door now!"

When the order had not been carried out fast enough, Aaron became desperate. He tried unsuccessfully to pound his way inside. Expletives shot from his mouth as he raged on like a sore loser at a racetrack. The title of "loser" suited him. He was a loser. One of the finest specimens of loser I'd ever met.

I shrugged off the onslaught of tears, tried to remain focused, even though the hope of saving Hannah's life was slipping away.

The bedroom door broke open. Aaron, Ann, and Renee entered.

"What in the—?" Aaron looked at Hannah, looked at my hands, looked at me. "You! Get off my daughter. Get away from her!"

"No one touches her," I said. "No one comes near her until medics arrive."

"What do you mean, medics?" Renee asked.

"Ma'am," the woman on the phone said, "What's happening? I'm going to need you to stay on the—"

"Not now," I shouted to the phone operator. "I don't mean any disrespect, but I need you to stop talking."

"Who is that?" Aaron demanded. "Who are you talking to? What's happened to Hannah? Why is she laying there? Why isn't she moving? Answer me!"

A terror-stricken Ann sagged to her daughter's side. "She's not … I mean, she's really not … breathing, Aaron."

Renee had been right to panic, to get in her car and drive here. Hannah had been in danger—only tonight, her biggest danger had been herself.

Aaron seized my waist with his hands, hurling my body to the side in one swift movement. My head smacked against the wall. I turned, watched Aaron toss Hannah around like a rag doll.

He was too late.

They all were.

There was no pulse.

No breath.

Her body was cold and tired.

She was gone.

CHAPTER 27

For the second time that day, I listened to the faint sound of sirens whine in the distance. Another minute or two and they would arrive, realize there was nothing they could do. Hannah was dead. She'd be zipped into a bag and carted away. It was a reality I couldn't allow myself to accept. Not when I'd done so little to save her.

"I'll meet the medics at the door when they get here." I tipped my head toward Aaron, hushed my voice, warned Renee. "Watch him. Don't let him touch anything. Not one thing. Got it?"

Her head bobbed up and down, though she was still in shock. We all were.

I staggered down the hall in a state of catatonia. The sirens were louder now, blazing in my ears. They were close. So close. Thirty minutes ago it might have meant something to me, might have given me hope. Now it meant nothing.

I hugged my arms around my body and squeezed. A single tear trailed down my cheek, its salty flavor stinging the edge of my chapped lips. I didn't wipe it away, I just let it puddle there. A text message came in from Cade. He asked how things were going. I stared at the words on the screen of my phone for a moment. When I couldn't produce anything logical to say, I shoved the phone back inside my pocket again.

My eyes caught the ruffled edge of the bottom of a flowery nightgown as it raced past me. Ann. Headed toward Hannah's room. Where had she been, and what was she doing scampering around?

I had one foot out the door ready to greet the ambulance when a piercing scream stopped me. The sound came from a woman. Whether that woman was Ann or Renee, I wasn't sure yet.

"You did this!" Ann yelled. "You killed her! My baby. My bay…bee!"

The realization was setting in.

"No, Ann," Renee yelled. "No! Stop it!"

Stop *what*?

I didn't walk back to Hannah's room—I ran, although nothing could have prepared me for the vision I beheld when I reentered the room. Aaron had dropped to one knee, his hand gripping the wood post at the end of Hannah's bed like it was a lifeline. His thin, white nightshirt was no longer white. It was red.

A bloody knife jutted from the end of Ann's hand.

"I … I …" Renee started when she saw me. "I tried to stop her, Sloane. I wanted to—"

"Ann, drop the knife," I said.

Keep calm. Don't freak out.

Aaron made no attempt to rise, no attempt to defend himself.

"Drop the knife!" I repeated. "Now!"

It was one of those surreal moments when, even though I didn't believe he should die, part of me almost wanted to see him get what was coming to him. There I was, standing over a man I hated, trying to save his miserable life.

Ann wielded her knife through the air, the tip pointed at Aaron. "Don't you see? Can't you see? It's *him*. It's all because of him. He did this! He took her from me! I'd rather waste away in jail for the rest of my life than see him get away with it."

She'd cracked, finally found the red button in her mind and pressed it, although I never thought it would happen like this. After years of abuse, a no-longer-timid Ann had exacted her revenge. Only her newfound strength had come too late to save her daughter.

As I caught sight of the medics ushering themselves down the hall, I swung, my hand grappling for the knife. Ann bounced back just in time, and my hand grasped nothing more than a fistful of air. I felt a stinging sensation and glanced down. My forearm was bleeding, dripping blood. In my attempt to recover the knife, Ann had sliced a five-inch cut into my skin. It wasn't deep, but that didn't stop the blood from gushing.

Ann's eyes widened, realizing her misstep. The jolt of reality was just what she needed. She straightened her hand, let the knife slip to the floor.

"Miss Monroe," she said. "I'm so sorry. I never meant to—"

"You didn't mean it, Ann. It's okay."

Three female medics entered the room, with a fourth, a male, close behind. The women glassed the room, took in the surroundings, stared at each other, didn't speak. The male took one step inside and backed out. "Let's go," he said while palming his phone, dialing. It wasn't hard to discern where they were going or who he was calling. The fact Aaron and I were injured was secondary to the threat posed by them being in a home that hadn't been secured. We had no choice. We'd have to sit and wait.

CHAPTER 28

"You three, don't move."

The order had been barked by a runty, yet muscular man wearing a navy windbreaker, jeans reminiscent of the mid-eighties, and multi-colored tennis shoes. A few minutes earlier he'd introduced himself as Proctor, said he was the captain of the Detectives Division. He had thick, dark circles under his eyes, and several strands of his peppery hair were askew. I almost had to interlock my fingers together to keep from reaching out and smoothing them back into place.

I didn't talk.

I didn't move.

I waited for the captain to ask his questions.

Waited for Cade to arrive.

In between the removal of Hannah and Aaron from the house, I'd managed a quick phone call while one of the medics attended to the laceration on my arm.

I didn't go into details, I just said I needed him. It was all I needed to say.

It was recommended that I go to the hospital to get checked out, even though there wasn't much wrong with me. I rebuffed the request. I'd seen enough of the inside of a hospital for one week.

Renee was crouched in the corner of the living room, sobbing. The waterworks had commenced when the paramedics arrived, and it didn't look like they'd be stopping anytime soon. I didn't blame her. A dead niece, a slave driver of a brother, a newly crazed sister-in-law. Even in the most dysfunctional of families, the week she was having trumped them all.

Ann sat on the edge of a reclining chair in an entirely different state of mind. Her eyes were glossed over, face stolid. All sense of emotion seemed to have ebbed from her body, having been replaced by a void I wasn't sure she'd ever bounce back from. If she had any regrets about stabbing her husband, it sure didn't seem like it.

It wasn't hard to determine how Hannah had reached a mental state where helplessness took over and suicide was her only way out. I sat with Proctor, Renee, and a handful of cops, the lot of us concentrating on Ann as she recalled the events leading up to Hannah's death. On the car ride from Jackson Hole to Idaho Falls,

Aaron had told Hannah he was moving her back home. For good. Hannah protested, saying he would no longer run her, no longer control her life. She was old enough to make her own decisions. This incited one of Aaron's epic fits of rage that continued long into the evening. In the end, when he wasn't getting what he wanted, he backed Hannah against the wall, repeatedly striking her in the face until she relented. He'd worn her down, as he had all the women in his life.

When Proctor questioned Ann about where she was when the physical abuse occurred, she said she was in the room, witnessing it all. His next question as to whether she made any attempt to intervene was met with a simple, regretful response. "Nothing. I did nothing."

Once Aaron had what he wanted, the plan he'd already decided upon was revealed. He would find Hannah the kind of job that would keep her close by, living at home, so he could monitor her every move. He didn't need her messing up again. He didn't need her disappointing him, "tainting" their wholesome family image more than she already had. Until further notice, she was on house arrest, only to be allowed out with his express permission. Boys were out of the question.

The weight of her bleak future had pushed Hannah to take a drastic measure. She was like a fragile bird who, after graduating, had been let out of the cage just long enough to get a taste of life before she was forced back into captivity. Hannah had pleaded, begged her father, even though she must have known in the end, it would all be for naught. Despondent, she saw one way out, one way to free herself—her mother's antidepressant pills. Ann had refilled the prescription only a day before, which meant since the bottle turned up empty, Hannah hadn't just swallowed a few … she'd swallowed them all.

When Ann finished, Proctor asked her to explain why she'd taken the knife to Aaron's back. It seemed like a ridiculous question to me. The motive couldn't have been more obvious, even to him. I quickly figured out his motive. He was baiting her, pressing her in a nonchalant way to admit what she'd done, confess to trying to kill, or maim, her husband.

Ann was unaffected. She clicked her wrists together, stuck them out toward Proctor. "What does it matter why I drove the knife into him? What does any of it matter now? I stabbed my husband. Twice. I hope he dies. Go ahead. Arrest me."

Proctor was taken aback by her frankness, allowing several seconds to pass before speaking. "Ma'am, I can feel your frustration from here. But why resort to such extreme measures?"

"He deserved it, that's why."

"You're admitting to the attempted murder of your husband?"

She nodded, her hands still gelled together in invisible handcuffs. "And just so *you* know, I would have finished the job if Miss Monroe hadn't stopped me. There's nothing you can do to me now that he hasn't already done. He's taken everything I care about and crushed it all—my hopes, my dreams, my sweet, innocent daughter. My life is over."

Proctor shook his head, tapped the shoulder of one of the officers in the room standing around like a misplaced piece of furniture. "Go on, take her in."

Ann stood, accepted her fate. Her hands were zip-tied behind her back, and she was led outside.

"Now," Proctor said. "Which one of you is Sloane Monroe?"

I lifted a finger.

He produced a clear, plastic baggie. Inside was a sliver of lined paper about the size of a rectangular refrigerator magnet. "How do you explain this?"

I bent down, recollected seeing the torn piece of paper in Hannah's notebook. "Where'd you find it?"

"Taped to the back of the ultrasound photo. Now answer the question."

I glanced at the words a second time, even though I didn't need to—they'd remain etched into my soul forever: *MISS MONROE: SAVE HIM. FIND HIM. BRING HIM HOME.*

"Who's she referring to?" Proctor prodded. "Who's *him*?"

"Her baby. I mean to say, the baby she gave up for adoption."

"What does the kid need saving from?"

"Several days ago, he was kidnapped."

Proctor scratched his head. "From who? Birth father or something?"

I shrugged. "We don't know yet."

"Are you talking about the AMBER Alert baby? The same kid that's been all over the news?"

I nodded. I wasn't in the mood to furnish him with the rest of the details, but I knew I wouldn't be allowed to leave until I pieced it all together for him, helped him grasp how I managed to end up at Aaron's house with Renee on the same night Hannah decided to end her life. I gave him a quick, five-minute recap, satisfying all his questions.

"This is one heck of a mess you got yourself here," he said.

My mess.

I suppose in a way, it was.

I'd gotten involved, agreed to help find Finn. Now, standing inside a house where I'd witnessed yet another innocent death, I doubted myself and my abilities, just like I had months before. I'd failed Hannah at every turn. She counted on me, asked me for one thing and one thing only—to find Finn—and I'd let her down. I felt responsible for her, for him, for all of it.

How could I save him?

I couldn't even save her.

CHAPTER 29

We arrived back at Cade's house at daybreak after a long ride home where I pretended to sleep, even though I hadn't slept a wink. I assumed Cade was well aware that I never dozed off. If he was, he never said anything. He just draped an arm around my shoulder and kept on driving.

Renee stayed behind to support Ann. The knife, which Ann managed to pierce Aaron with not once, but twice, had passed through the cavities in his ribs, causing one of his lungs to collapse. He also sustained a severed artery. Injuries aside, he'd live long enough to press charges against Ann for attempted murder, which was exactly what he said he intended to do, along with filing for a divorce. I wonder what he thought of his perfect family now.

I showered and changed into something I could lounge in. Sleep wasn't an option. Even if I could calm my nerves enough to catch a wink or two, I never napped in the middle of the day.

I found Cade in the kitchen whipping up a batch of steel-cut oats. For such a tough guy, he sure knew his way around a kitchen.

"Can I make you somethin' to eat?" he asked.

I shook my head.

"Thanks, I'm fine."

"When was the last time you ate?"

Good question. Lunch the day before. On the downside, I was starving, but my stomach was unsettled. On the upside, it felt like I'd shed a few pounds in the last couple days. Not that I needed it, but I didn't know a woman on earth who was opposed to a fair amount of weight loss.

"I'll eat, just not right now."

He pulled up a chair, sat beside me. "You doin' okay?"

I didn't know what "okay" felt like anymore. The very notion was fleeting. It burst into my life, taunting me with a sense of calm and serenity before withdrawing again.

"No, I'm not."

"Do you want to talk about it?" he asked.

"No."

"You know what happened with Hannah wasn't your fault, right?"

I didn't respond. I couldn't respond. I wasn't sure what to say. There was a good chance any discussion about Hannah would lead to tears, an emotion I had no interest stirring up after I'd worked so diligently the last few hours to tuck it away.

We sat in silence, absorbed the moment together. Cade rubbed a hand along my leg. He looked distraught, like he longed to lift my spirits. Remaining by my side helped more than he could ever know. I wanted to tell him. I couldn't do that either.

Cade glanced at a horseshoe-shaped clock on the wall made of barn wood. "I better get showered."

"Where are you going?"

"Serena's funeral is today."

The last twenty-four hours had been so astonishing, the funeral had fled my mind.

"We can talk again later, after I get back," he continued, "… that is, if you decide you want to. No pressure."

He slipped off the stool, leaned in like he was about to embrace me, gave my back a quick scratch instead.

"Wait a minute," I said. "I'd like to go. I mean, would it be all right with you if I went?"

"'Course it would. I didn't mean to make you feel like I didn't want you there. I just assumed you needed some rest, maybe some time to yourself. I know what it's like to need a breather."

Rest. I probably needed it. I just didn't want it.

CHAPTER 30

I sat in a rectangular-shaped, oak pew next to Cade and Shelby. I'd dressed in a charcoal-colored, button-up shirt I had in my suitcase and a black skirt that belonged to Shelby. The skirt could have been an inch or two longer. Under the circumstances, I didn't have much choice.

As far as ceremonies go, Serena's was one of the loveliest I'd attended. We arrived to the soft melody of a harp, played by a teenage boy sitting in the far corner in the back. The service started with a couple musical numbers, one by a small group of Serena's nieces and nephews, and another, a ballad, sung by a woman who had the chops to headline a show on Broadway. Serena's father presided, giving a spiritual, heartfelt speech that left most people in the room uplifted instead of in tears.

At the end of his speech, Serena's father invited attendees to come up to the front and share a memory, a thought, a sentiment of some kind. A handful of people lined up to express their gratitude, including Wendy, who, up until that moment, I had no idea was in attendance. And I wasn't the only one. Cade tensed at the sight of her. Others who knew who she was held a hand to their mouths, shocked to see she was back in town. And those who weren't shocked couldn't tear their eyes away from her puffy, black eye, courtesy of her hotel beating the day before.

Wendy was dressed in a rainbow of colors, donning a paisley dress that made my skirt look long and her look like a hippie. Paired with five-inch wedge shoes and clunky metal jewelry, she looked like a celebrity who'd just incurred a fine on TV's *Fashion Police*.

Cade struggled to remain composed. "What's she doing here?"

"She did say she was coming."

"I made it clear she was to stay away from my family—from the funeral. She knows being here is a bad idea."

Only, I wasn't sure she did.

"She heard and understood you. She just doesn't care."

And it was too late to stop her now.

Wendy stepped up to the microphone and scanned the crowd, pausing long enough to appraise the mixed reactions on everyone's faces, from those who didn't know her, to those who knew her all too well. She beamed a broad smile around the room, seeming unruffled by the attention. Cade's Aunt Bonnie, who was next in line to speak, looked like she wanted to pluck the amplifier from Wendy's hands and blacken her other eye with it.

"For those of you who don't know me, my name is Wendy McCoy. I mean, well, it's actually Wendy Smart McCoy Sanders. I just haven't made it to the courthouse to change it back again."

Smart had to have been the most ironic maiden name for this woman ever. At least she had the "smarts" to admit she was no longer married to Cade.

"Anyway, I knew Serena," she continued, "and I just wanted to say that although we weren't as close at the end of her life as I wanted to be, we were close at the beginning. Well, not the beginning … the middle, I guess you could say. I met her when I was dating my … umm … when I was with Cade, and we got to be good friends."

Just in case anyone was unfamiliar with the Cade she was referring to, she didn't just look in his direction, she waved at him. I thought I was going to need to find him a paper bag to breathe into.

"Serena accepted me," Wendy said. "She always treated me like I was her equal, no matter how many times I screwed up. Most of you don't know I kept in touch with her over the years. Not a lot, a few phone conversations here and there. I wanted to stand up here today and publicly say how much I'll miss her."

Wendy's speech, even with its flawed, and at times, laugh-out-loud moments, had turned out better than I pictured in my mind. If only that had been the end of it.

"A couple weeks ago I was in a bad place in my life," Wendy continued, "and I reached out to the only person I knew I could trust. Serena gave me some great advice. I took her advice, and now I'm standing here today. Alive and free. Mourning not only a friend, but the unborn baby she was carrying."

The words "unborn baby" tore through the room, igniting an audible gasp that reverberated across the crowd. It was like a bomb had detonated, and I was waiting for the dust to settle so I could gauge how many people had been affected, how much damage she'd done. In seconds it became obvious everyone heard and understood what Wendy had said. Whispers began, everyone wondering why they'd been kept in the dark about Serena's pregnancy.

Feeling responsible for Wendy's verbal blunder, Cade started to rise until Bonnie took a few steps toward Wendy and said, "You've had your turn, Wendy. There are many others waiting for the opportunity to have their say."

"I wasn't finished," Wendy said. "There's no time limit on these things, Bonnie."

"You are finished."

The words "you are finished" were spoken with a kind of quiet respect, but they hadn't been voiced by Bonnie. They'd been uttered by Jack. He sat in the front row, his head down, hands cupping both sides of his face.

"Jack," Wendy pleaded. "There's so much more I want to say. I was just—"

"I have to put a stop to this," Cade said. "It will only get worse."

An otherwise flawless ceremony had taken a scandalous turn. It was disheartening. If only Wendy could have been spotted at the beginning, before she had the chance to wreak irreversible havoc.

A tearful, visibly shamed Shelby stood, looked Wendy in the eyes. "Mom, you need to leave."

Wendy froze, still blissfully unaware of what she'd done wrong.

With Shelby *falling* apart and Cade about to *tear* Wendy apart, I attempted to fix the situation in the only way I knew how. I walked to the front, leaned in, and whispered, "Come on, Wendy. Let me walk you out."

She shrugged me off. "No … I …"

"If you cared for Serena as you say you did, come with me. Please."

She was lucky. I didn't hand out "pleases" often, but in that moment, I was prepared to beg her if it meant sparing Serena's family any further humiliation.

Reluctant, yet seeing she was in over her head in a way she didn't fathom, the two of us did the "Wendy walk of shame." All eyes followed us down the aisle and through the double doors until we reached the main courtyard outside, shielded from everyone's line of sight.

"I didn't do anything wrong," Wendy started. "I'm so tired of people pointing the finger, blaming everything on me. Not everything I do is my fault, you know."

"Wendy."

"I mean it. I'm sick of it. I'm not going to allow—"

"Wendy!"

She stood, feet apart, hands on hips. "What?"

"Shut … up!"

"You know something? You're freaking rude."

I attempted to find even the smallest shred of Zen balance that would keep me from killing the woman I'd saved only a day before. "The last day has been challenging for me. I need you to put a muzzle on it for one minute and hear what I have to say. If you can do that, I'll explain why everyone was trying to stop you in there. If you can't, I'll put you in my car and we'll drive away. You won't talk to anyone else here, you won't see anyone else here."

She flung her head from side to side thinking about it. "I … guess that sounds fair."

I didn't waste any time. I dug right in.

"Besides Jack, Cade, Grace, and myself, no one knew Serena was pregnant."

I stood there, hoping it would sink in without me having to draw a diagram to explain the ripple effect she'd just caused. The light in her head, if there was one, switched on and off and back on again.

"I didn't know," she muttered. "I swear."

"I believe you. I truly don't believe you would have said anything if you did."

"Serena never told me it was a secret."

"She probably never expected her own funeral either, with you in attendance and talking about it before she and Jack had the chance to tell everyone themselves."

"Why didn't they tell anyone?"

"Serena died before she had the chance. Jack is too grieved to talk about it right now. He asked Cade to keep it a secret until he was ready to share it with everyone."

She placed her hands on her hips, turned away from me, her voice unstable. "I screw everything up, you know? No matter how many times I think I'm doing the right thing, I always manage to get it wrong."

"You're not alone, believe me."

She snorted a laugh. "You? Are you kidding? You probably haven't made a misstep in your entire, perfect life."

She was wrong in ways she'd never understand. I wasn't about to enlighten her.

"I think it's best for you and everyone else if you leave before the reception. I'm not saying that because I want to keep you from Cade. I just think you being here after what just happened isn't the best idea."

"You must hate me, for coming back to Jackson, dragging up the past," she said. "And yet you saved my life. Why?"

"I don't hate you, Wendy, and I have no right to judge you. I saved your life because it was the right thing to do."

"The right thing … I've heard that exact phrase before from Cade. Look, it's not easy for me to say this, but you seem good for him. When he looks at you, he looks happy, like he's found what he wants in life. Treat him right, okay? Don't break his heart. He's too good of a person to have it happen twice in a lifetime."

"First you don't want me to be with him, and now you do?"

"When Cade came to see me last night at the hospital, we talked, not long, just long enough for me to be honest with myself. The way he talks to me—it's like he's a robot. No emotion. He doesn't love me anymore. He loves you. So, I'm leaving. Right now, actually. I planned on telling him after the funeral."

"Where will you go?"

"I'm headed back east for a while, moving in with my sister. We talked last night for the first time in a long time. She invited me to stay with her, help me get things together. It's time I straighten my life out. Besides, it's best for everyone if I go. Say goodbye for me, okay?"

"No, Wendy, wait. It wouldn't be best for *everyone* if you left like this. You walked out on Shelby's life once without saying goodbye. She's your daughter. Don't let it happen a second time. If you ever want her to find it in her heart to forgive you for what happened, you can start by not repeating the same missteps you made in the past."

Twenty minutes later, I stood by Cade's side, watched Shelby walk Wendy to her car. Words were exchanged, and the conversation was civil, for once. Shelby hugged Wendy goodbye, even managed a small grin. As much as Shelby wanted to hate her, I knew deep down the pain of desertion had caused her suffering. However flawed Wendy was, a part of Shelby would always yearn to have her in her life.

Cade stood behind me, his hands running up and down my arms. "You know somethin'? You're one hell of a woman."

CHAPTER 31

I woke the next morning curled into a fetal position on the floor of the room I'd been sleeping in for the past several days. I didn't know how I got there, how long I'd been there, or why. Someone had covered me with a fleece blanket and tucked a pillow under my head. The last thing I remembered was sitting by the fire next to Cade the night before, indulging in a glass of wine, talking about … *what was it we talked about?* I couldn't remember.

"You're awake."

I surveyed the room, jumped when I noticed Cade sitting on a rocking chair a few feet behind me.

"How … long have you been sitting there?" I asked.

"I slept here."

"In the chair? All night?"

I didn't know whether to feel creeped out, appreciative, or like a complete idiot. Currently, I was sure I was exhibiting all three emotions simultaneously. Before I could ask why he was there or why he felt the need to watch over me, he answered my concerns by stating, "You screamed in your sleep last night."

I propped a pillow behind me on the wall, scooted back onto it. "No, I didn't."

"Sloane, you did."

"Maybe it wasn't me you heard. Maybe it was Shelby."

"Wasn't me," Shelby leaned against the door jamb, yawned while she was talking. "I'm the one who told him you were screaming."

"Great, you both heard me?"

Somehow I'd managed to get out of bed, scream loud enough for Shelby to hear, and not remember any of it. I looked at the bed. It was still made from the day before. There was one thing out of place, a lumpy area in the middle, leading me to believe at one point I'd laid on top of it, or set on top of it, at least.

"I came to see what all the fuss was about and found you on the floor," Shelby said. "You'd stopped screaming, and your eyes were closed like you were sleeping. I didn't know what to do, so I got my dad."

"Thank you, Shelby. I'm sorry for waking you. I don't think I've ever done that before."

Shelby looked at Cade, gnawed on the outside of her bottom lip. "Why were you screaming?"

"I don't know," I said. "I don't even remember it."

"Bonnie's here," Cade said.

Great. Does she know too? Does everyone? Is this how it works in this family?

"What's she doing here?" I asked.

Cade and Shelby exchanged glances again. Neither spoke.

"What's wrong?" I asked. "Is it Jack? Is he okay? Finn? Is there news?"

I couldn't handle hearing about another tragedy. Not now.

"Everything's fine," Cade said. "And there's nothin' new on Finn as far as I know."

Shelby backed out of the room without saying another word and disappeared down the hall.

"What's going on?" I asked.

Bonnie tapped on the outside of my open door then poked her head inside. "Cade, Harold's here to see you."

"The chief?" I asked. "Will someone please tell me what's going on?"

Cade looked at me. "Like I said, everything's fine. I'll be right back."

I'd hoped Bonnie would close the door behind her, allowing me to conceal what little dignity I had left. She didn't. She stood there, smiling down at me. Staring.

"What do you say we take a walk?" she suggested.

Taking a walk on a brisk, fall morning was the last thing I wanted to do right now. I needed a long, hot soak in the bathtub.

"I'm not dressed or ready to go out yet, Bonnie. Another day?"

Bonnie raised the blanket with a few fingers, assessed my attire. "You're wearing pants and a tank top. You look plenty dressed to me." She held out a hand. "Up you go."

...

I had my hoodie tied in a bow so tight around my face, only my eyes and the top part of my nose stuck out. And yet, my face didn't feel warmer, not even a tiny bit. The cool breeze managed to slip through the cracks, blasting me with shots of ice-cold air until I couldn't feel my face anymore. Bonnie, on the other hand, was dressed in a T-shirt and Capri pants, prancing around like it was the middle of summer.

"I just love days like this," Bonnie said. "Sun out, leaves a multitude of different colors. I bet you couldn't find fresher mountain air if you tried."

Right now the only thing I wanted to *find* was a heat source.

"What are you doing here?" I asked. "And why do I have the impression it has something to do with me?"

"You get right to the point, don't you?"

"I don't mean to seem—"

"You're not, hun. I like you just the way you are, fiery spirit and all. You're direct, no-nonsense. Wish more women in my life were that way. To answer your question, I did come here to talk to you."

"Why?"

"Cade called me. I know what happened to the girl, Hannah. I also know about your outburst last night. Question is, do *you* remember it?"

"Screaming? No. Let me guess. You're here because he's worried. I'm fine, Bonnie. I appreciate your concern, but I don't need—"

"Therapy?"

Therapy? I was going to say advice. Was she suggesting I book an appointment with her daughter?

"I appreciate the offer, but I don't think talking to Grace is a good idea."

"I never suggested you talk to Grace."

"What are you suggesting then?"

"For today, why not talk to me?"

"We are talking. Isn't that why we're out here, to talk?"

I was doing everything in my power to keep my anxiety from bubbling over like an unattended kettle on the stove. Bonnie reached out, felt my hand. "My, you're freezing! I have to apologize. I didn't even stop to think you might not be as warm-blooded as I am. Let's get you back inside."

Although I felt like a weakling, I made no objections.

The chief had come and gone by the time we returned. Not knowing why he'd stopped by, yet again, bothered me. Until I could shake free of Bonnie, the mystery of his visit would have to wait.

Cade and Shelby were talking in the dining room when we walked in.

"You two, out," Bonnie demanded.

"Out?" Cade asked.

"That's what I said, Cade. Take Shelby and grab some hot cocoa somewhere. Sloane and I have a conversation to finish. I don't need long. A few minutes should do it."

"We can talk another—"

"Nonsense," Bonnie replied to me. "We'll finish now."

Three minutes later, we were alone, sitting beside one another on the couch.

"Grace is an accomplished therapist. And …" Bonnie winked, "she happened to learn from the best."

"You're *both* therapists?" I finally understood what she was doing here and why. "Therapy isn't my thing."

She placed a hand on her hip. Frowned. "How do you know? Have you ever tried it?"

"Do you talk to all of your patients this way?"

"You're not my patient. Besides, I'm not practicing anymore. I retired last year."

I stood, turned. "I'm not comfortable discussing my personal life with you. I yelled in my sleep one time. So what? I don't deserve to sit here and be interrogated over it. I never asked for your advice."

"Three times."

I whipped around. "Excuse me?"

"Last night was the third time you've screamed in the middle of the night since you've been here."

"It doesn't make sense. I've never had this problem before."

"Actually, you have, hun," Bonnie said. "Shelby told Cade when she stayed at your house last year, you did it then too. Just the one night though."

I lowered myself back onto my spot on the sofa, let her words marinate, tried to accept what she was suggesting, even though I didn't want to believe it was real.

"I tend to believe listening is what I do best," she said. "And you can talk to me anytime about anything. My door's always open to you. That said, I understand the level of discomfort you might have talking to a relation of Cade's. I came here to offer you the number of a good friend of mine instead."

She dug inside her pocket, held out a folded slip of paper. "Don't put up a fight, and don't refuse the number and say you won't go. Take it. Whether you choose to find a way past your troubles or not is up to you. You seem like an amazing woman, Sloane. Don't make the blunder of deciding therapy will take that away from you. If you embrace it, it has the power to change your life in ways you can't imagine."

CHAPTER 32

Teresa Foster was tiny, the kind of tiny that, at first, made me suspect she led a life of clean eating, consuming nothing but fruits, vegetables, and green smoothies. And yet she had a half-eaten cherry pie sitting on her desk with a fork sticking out of it. Why bother with a plate when you can dig right in?

I'd arrived at the Precious Gift Adoption Agency alone, having told Cade I needed the day to myself. I needed a breather, a moment to get centered, to focus on the task at hand. I hadn't had any "me time" for days. Making myself useful seemed like the only way to drive the repeated visions of Hannah's death from my head.

Cade never asked where I was going or about my conversation with Bonnie. He just nodded and said he'd come to a kind of truce with the chief, who had just learned of Hannah's suicide. The sand had slowly sifted through the hourglass until there was nothing left except lost time. If Finn wasn't found within the next week, the chief would retire, having gone out with an unsolved case on his hands. This left him with humble desperation, willing to accept help anywhere he could get it in order to wrap the case up, retire with a clear conscience. Even if solving it led to the kind of grizzly outcome no one was prepared to accept, it would bring the kind of closure he so desperately wanted.

The chief had even extended a small courtesy to me, telling Cade he'd allow me to provide assistance if I stayed out of everyone's way. Out of the way to me meant out of sight. I accepted the olive branch, deciding I'd do everything in my power to make today count, starting with Teresa Foster. While I talked to her, Cade drove to the home of Miguel Alvarez. If his wife hadn't learned the truth by now, she was about to be enlightened.

I looked at Teresa. "You were the one who worked with Serena and Jack on finding them a baby, correct?"

Teresa sectioned off a mouthful of pie and took a bite, allowing flakes from the crust to pepper her desk, joining the other casualties that had previously fallen by the wayside. I'd cordoned off the section of the desktop in front of me, and was a couple seconds away from suggesting she allow me to clear hers as well before I stopped myself.

"We've never had anything happen like this before at Precious Gift. We've been helping prospective parents adopt babies for the last nineteen years. We have an impeccable track record. We successfully match eighty-nine percent of our families in the first eighteen months, and fifty-five percent within the first twelve."

What a perfectly orchestrated speech. Apparently she thought I was a candidate.

"You didn't answer my question."

"Oh, right. I'm not supposed to talk about my clients. You know, confidentiality and all." She grabbed a packet out of a drawer, flopped it down on the desk, interlaced her hands on top of it. "Now, as I said on the phone, the application fee is $750 and your first deposit will be $8,000. I'll need both amounts before we can place your profile on our website and start showing you to potential birth parents."

"Who exactly do you think I am?" I asked.

"Mrs. Redmond. We spoke on the phone about an hour ago. Right?"

"Wrong."

I took out one of my cards, used my pointer finger to slide it over to her, watched her eyes expand when she read the words "Private Investigator."

"Oh. Oh my. I probably shouldn't be talking to you."

"Why?" I asked. "Haven't you already spoken to the police?"

"They asked me a few questions. I'm sure I wasn't much help. I have no idea what happened to that baby or why our agency was targeted."

"Targeted? What makes you think your agency is part of this?"

She squeezed her eyes closed like she wanted to regurgitate what she'd just said. "Oops. Poor choice of words. What I meant to say is, we look at our clients as family, so an attack on them is an attack on us."

I rapped my fingers along the edge of the desk, tried to decide whether her explanation had been a quick save or if there was a remote chance she was as innocent as her button-up, flowered dress suggested. She fidgeted with a pencil, flipping it around and around in her hand like she was helpless to make it stop.

"Were you at the hospital when Hannah gave birth to the baby?" I asked.

She nodded.

"I was there to witness Hannah sign the adoption consent form."

"Did you have any problems getting her to sign?"

"Hannah hesitated for a few minutes when I gave it to her. I wondered if she'd changed her mind, until her aunt reassured her."

"After she signed, what happened?" I asked.

"Like I said, I told all of this to the police already."

"Doesn't hurt saying it one more time then, right?"

She glanced around the room. Seeing no one, she continued. "After Hannah signed, she kissed the baby and handed him to her aunt. Her aunt took him to Jack and Serena, who were waiting in the hall."

"While you were there, did anything unusual happen? Anything out of the ordinary?"

"Like what?"

"Any people there that shouldn't have been? Any family members who weren't supposed to know about the adoption and found out somehow?"

"Besides the aunt and the Westwoods, no other visitors stopped by to see Hannah. Not while I was there, at least."

"What about phone calls?" I asked. "Did Hannah get any calls?"

"If she had a phone with her, I never saw it. After the baby was born, I didn't stay long. It was busy that night."

"Busy how?"

"There were more people on the maternity ward than usual. More than I'd ever seen in any of my previous visits."

"Why?" I asked.

"It was like every woman who was due that week had spontaneously gone into labor on the same night. There was another woman who had so many visitors coming and going, the doctor on call started sending them away so they wouldn't disturb the other patients."

"So it's possible someone could have been there, for Hannah, and you may not have noticed?"

She shrugged. "Guess so."

"This other family you mentioned, do you happen to know their names?"

"Well, I do. I probably shouldn't—"

"Giving me the name isn't going to hurt anything. The other family isn't your client."

Wearing her down had been easy so far, I figured, why not keep pushing?

"I … guess you're right. Besides, they made a big splash of it by announcing the birth of their baby on the front page of the paper, so it's public knowledge anyway."

"I take it they're someone well known around here then?"

She nodded.

"Mayor Bronson and his wife." Teresa glanced to the side, flinching when she spied a man making a beeline in our direction. "I can't say anymore. Really, I can't."

The man stuck out his hand well before he reached me. "Lyle Smith. Manager. How are things going here?"

He was tall and had the bone structure and swagger of a person I imagined gave motivational speeches for a living.

"Sloane. Client. Fine."

"What, no last name?" He laughed at what I presumed he thought was a witty remark until neither one of us joined in. He then cleared his throat into the center of his balled-up fist and tried to recover. "Anything I can help with, questions I can answer?"

The pencil Teresa had been fidgeting with came to an abrupt halt. It nose-dived from her hand, making a tinging sound when it hit the desk. She snatched it up, shoved it back inside the drawer.

I stood.

"I think I have all the information I need." I held my hand out toward Teresa. "I almost left here without my packet."

"Right."

She placed it into my hand, did her best to play along, act natural, even though her hand was visibly shaking when she handed it to me.

"I'll talk this over with my husband tonight and get back to you."

"I look forward to hearing from you," Teresa said, even though it was obvious she hoped to never see me again.

"I hope you'll consider Precious Gift," Lyle added. "We'd love to help you and your husband find your baby."

Find my baby.

A baby for me.

For a moment, I almost forgot it had all been a charade.

CHAPTER 33

The Bronson residence was located at the end of a private road surrounded by an array of quaking aspen and pine trees. The set-up made the property and its vast surroundings look like a fortress, probably because it was one. All that was missing was a guard at the gate.

I passed through the entrance, driving in between two massive wood logs, hoisted at least fifteen feet in the air. A third log was nailed across the top, framing the outside. A three-foot-wide metal sign was suspended from the center. The sign had an etched nature landscape along the edges, and in the center, the name BRONSON was presented in capital letters. Although the primitive nature of the sign wasn't my taste, it was a spectacular display for a family who lived on a spectacular piece of prime Jackson Hole real estate.

At first glance, the ranch-style home stretched out so wide on both sides, it looked like two or three houses next to each other with shared common walls. A double door in the middle indicated it was a single residence. The front door opened before I stepped out of my car. The Bronsons lived at the end of a private drive, and I wasn't expected. A man walked toward me, leaving a woman hovering in the doorway, her curious eyes fixed on me.

While the woman didn't look much older than thirty, I guessed the man was pushing fifty. He had unruly, sand-colored hair and a trimmed beard. When he half-grinned at me, I noticed one of his eyes was slightly bigger than the other, or maybe it just looked that way because one was circular in shape and the other was shaped more like a leaf. Eye shape aside, he reminded me of a younger version of Clint Eastwood, and I couldn't stop staring.

"Can I help you?" he asked.

"Mayor Bronson?"

"That's right."

He had a raspy, yet pleasant tone.

"My name is—"

He held up a hand, stopping me. "No need, Miss Monroe. I know who you are, and I know why you're here."

"You do?"

I couldn't see how. I hadn't told anyone I was coming.

"Is there anything you don't involve yourself in?" he asked.

"I take it you're friends with Chief Rollins."

Mayor Bronson came to a stop a couple feet in front of me, feet shoulder-width apart, arms crossed tight in front of his denim, button-up shirt. "I know Harold. Why?"

"Can I talk to you about the night your wife gave birth? I understand she delivered the same night Hannah Kinkade did."

"She did."

"I was told there was a lot of traffic on the maternity ward that night."

"By whom?"

"Doesn't matter, does it?"

He cocked his head to one side, squinted like he was trying to decide what he thought of me. "S'pose not."

Mayor Bronson's wife approached from behind. "Colt, who's this?"

"My name is Sloane Monroe," I said.

She smiled. "I'm Lizzy. You were the one who found those girls last year, right?"

I nodded.

"Are you helping find the missing baby?"

"Trying to," I said. "That's why I'm here. I was hoping I could talk to you about the night you were in the hospital."

Before I could say anything more, a familiar truck turned up the drive. It came to a stop a couple feet away, and the window went down.

"Sloane, what brings you here?" Chief Rollins asked.

I didn't answer.

Mayor Bronson nodded at the chief then looked at me. "Look, Miss Monroe. We've already sat down with Harold, told him everything there is to know. I think it's best you try a different approach."

Precisely what I was trying to do.

"I respect your opinion, Mayor, but I don't agree."

"Why's that?"

"I've thought a lot about this case over the last few days, and I've come to realize something."

"Go on."

"This entire time, I've based my theories about the kidnapping on statistics, knowing in similar cases, most signs point to a friend or family member. What if we're going about this all wrong? What if the person that took Finn wasn't someone who knew Hannah was pregnant or knew the Westwoods were adopting?"

"What are you suggesting?" he asked.

"I'm suggesting it was someone outside both family circles. A stranger."

"We've considered all possible motives and suspects, Miss Monroe," the chief said.

"What proof do you have to back your theory?" Mayor Bronson asked.

"None. Yet."

The mayor draped an arm around his wife, kissed her on the cheek, and walked to the passenger side of the chief's truck, pausing before he got in. "Take it up with the chief when you do."

"Mayor Bronson, if you'd just allow me to ask a few questions, I'd really—"

"Proof first, Miss Monroe. I'm a busy man."

I stood, watching the truck roll back down the road, my hope for a good lead rolling away with it. Halfway to the front entrance, the truck slowed. It seemed the mayor had anticipated my next move just in time, realizing with him gone, I'd attempt to strike up the same conversation with Lizzy. He was right. I would have.

"I'm sorry," Lizzy said. "I wish I could answer your questions."

I appreciated the sentiment, but I wasn't satisfied. And I wasn't about to finish the day without some definitive answers.

CHAPTER 34

I drove about four or five minutes before I felt it, an overwhelming sense of fear and helplessness. Failure. It started the same way it always did, a seed of discord inside my stomach, growing at an accelerated rate, like it had been stimulated with rich fertilizer. If I didn't calm it down, if I didn't tame it, I knew what would happen next. It would consume me, explode into an attack that would bring my search for Finn to a screeching halt.

I'd experienced the sensation off and on since I was a child, my earliest recollection being the first time I watched my drunken father take a swing at my mother. His powerful fist had connected with precision, dislodging one of her teeth. It shot across the room, plopping down on the carpet in front of me. My father turned my direction, saw me hunched in a ball in the corner, peeking at my mother, peeking at him. The fact I was out of bed when I wasn't supposed to be angered him all the more. I can still hear the sound of his footsteps as he approached me, raising his hand once more. I braced for impact, accepted my punishment, until the saving grace of my mother flung herself in front of me, shielding me with her body.

The fear. The anxiety. The helplessness. At the tender age of seven, I was too young to be conscious of what I was feeling or why. I just knew I didn't feel right. I felt sick inside, and I didn't know how to make myself better.

I relied on instinct. I knew I needed to protect my mother, my sister Gabby. Five years later, with help from a baseball bat, I did. That's the day I became strong. That's the day I hardened. Maybe it was even the reason why I'd always sabotaged my relationships with men. Or why I picked the wrong men. Or why I pushed the right ones away. My father had been the poorest possible example of a loving husband and father, leaving me with nothing but the kind of acidy taste in my mouth I'd never been able to wash out.

Over the years, I'd learned how to spin my bouts of anxiety into strength, suppress the negative memories, and focus on the positive ones. It worked most of the time, until something triggered my past, and then it all came flooding back again in one long, perpetual flashback. Every life. Every death. Every success. Every failure.

I jerked the steering wheel, pulled the car to the side of the road, closed my eyes, and practiced my breathing. Sometimes it worked. Other times, like now, it didn't. My lungs tightened, and as I struggled for even the smallest of breaths, I embraced my anguish, took out my phone, and dialed.

CHAPTER 35

I sat in a room painted a soft, eggshell blue, staring at a variety of framed Monet knockoffs hung in groups of three on every wall except one. Very precise. Very organized. The simplistic perfection should have put me at ease. It was the exact kind of room I lived for—everything in its place—and yet I longed to be outside the office again.

I tapped the toe of my shoe on the smooth, gray rug and contemplated what I was doing here and why. I felt better now. Over the past several minutes, I'd managed to ease some of my tension, reverse my inner turmoil until it was almost the size of a seed again.

Deciding my decision was made in haste, I stood up as the door to the left of me opened. A teenager stared at the ground, her hands in her pockets as she passed me. Another woman, who looked to be in her late thirties, stood in the doorway. I turned, thinking I'd walk out behind the teenager, even though I was well aware it was too late.

"Sloane?"

I addressed the woman speaking to me with a nod. Dressed in a tank top, a long, colorful maxi skirt, and sandals, she wasn't anything like what I envisioned a shrink would be. Her hair was fashioned in a loose ponytail, and her face, while devoid of makeup, had such a bright complexion, she didn't need any.

"Hi, I'm Elodie. Come on in."

I entered her office expecting to see a leather sofa, brown, with pleated, oversized circles pressed into the cushion. There wasn't one. Instead, I was met with a simple couch. A loveseat. Beige, just like the color of the walls in her office. The couch was small, simple. Not quite big enough for two, although I guessed some couples squished together anyway in a forced display of affection.

Elodie sat behind a desk across from me. She turned a page in her notebook, rested it on her lap.

"What brings you here today?"

What brought me in was a moment of crisis and the fact she'd had a sudden cancellation.

"Bonnie referred me to you. She thought it would be good to sit down, talk some things out. Now that I'm here, I feel fine. And I don't want to waste your time."

"You're not wasting my time," she said. "I'm glad you came in."

Given her hourly rate, I'm sure she was thrilled.

We stared at each other for a while. I felt as though she was waiting for me to speak, even though I had no idea what to say to a person I knew nothing about. The fact she was a shrink and dealt with this all the time meant nothing to me.

"What made you decide to call me today?" she asked.

"I was driving and I felt … anxious. It happens to me sometimes. I deal with it until it passes, and then I'm fine."

How many others had sat where I was now sitting, downplaying their own situations?

"How did the anxiety begin?" she asked. "What I mean to say is—what happened to bring it on today?"

"Have you ever woken up in the morning, thought about your life, and felt like no matter what efforts you make to move forward, to make a difference, to do something good, you can't stop repeating the same mistakes over and over?"

Perfect. Now I was shrinking the shrink.

"Do you feel like you're repeating mistakes over and over?" she asked.

It occurred to me I wasn't getting out of here without revealing something meaningful about myself, and I had another fifty minutes to go. Better start talking.

"I'm not sleeping."

"When did it start? Do you remember?"

Of course I remembered.

"When my sister died."

"How long ago was this?" she asked.

"Several years ago."

"What happened?"

"She was murdered by a serial killer."

"That must have been very difficult for you."

She looked like she was making every effort to maintain neutral on her true feelings about my confession.

"Instead of finding ways to get past it, I spent my nights consumed with rage, focusing every waking moment on how I could find her killer, make him pay for what he did." I bet that wasn't something she heard every day. "A few years later, when he started his killing spree again, I found him. And I killed him. Well, he didn't die by my hand, but he's dead."

"Did his death help you find the closure you wanted?"

"In some ways."

"And in other ways?"

"I've seen things in my life," I said. "Too many things."

"Such as?"

"Abuse."

"What else?"

"Death. The kind of death that happens on purpose, not by accident. I've witnessed it firsthand with cases I've worked on. Sometimes I've even been there when it happened."

She leaned back, pressed her legs together. I imagined she sat day after day, listening to the same mundane problems. Not today. Not with me. Her facial expression changed. She actually looked *interested*.

"You watched someone die?"

"Not someone, lots of someones."

This sparked a series of questions about my profession and my life, past and present. Questions that would have taken a handful of sessions to get through. Questions I didn't want to answer. I touched on the highlights, gave minor details, watched the minutes tick by on my cell phone. Twenty more to go, and I was out of here. She asked what brought me to Jackson Hole. I told her. I also explained the reason I hadn't left yet. One of them anyway.

"How does it feel to work on a new case after taking a break for so many months?"

"I thought it would feel great," I said. "Thought it would give me focus, help me get past the slump I was in."

"And has it?"

Given the fact I was sitting in front of her, having suffered a panic attack less than two hours before, the question answered itself.

"I don't know."

"Tell me about your anxiety. What happens when you feel a panic attack coming on?"

"I try to catch my breath, meditate, breathe my way through it."

"Good. Do you feel the breathing helps you?"

"Sometimes."

"What have you done in the past when it doesn't?"

"I have a prescription," I said.

"For?"

"Xanax."

She raised a brow. "Does it help?"

"Faster than trying to work it out on my own."

"How often do you take it?"

"Maybe one every four to six months."

She didn't like my answer.

"When we were talking earlier about these attacks, you said you've had several in the past six months—ever since your friend Carlo died. You didn't take Xanax then?"

"I didn't want to."

"Why?"

"Taking it makes me feel … I don't know. Like there's something wrong with me."

There was something wrong with me. Clearly.

She jotted several words down on a notepad. "So, even though you know it helps you, you're uncomfortable taking it?"

"I'd rather try calming myself down another way first."

"Look at it like this—it's meant to help you. You don't take it all the time, and you don't abuse it. Taking something that helps you doesn't make you any less of a person. It means you care enough about yourself and your wellbeing to do what's right for you."

"I don't want medication to come between my ability to be successful at what I do. I feel like it slows me down."

"Is slowing down a bad thing?"

Considering the rapid rate in which I liked to do things, I always assumcd it was.

Elodie glanced at a clock on her desk. "Do you like to read?"

"Not really. Why?"

"Our time is about up. I'd like to give you an assignment. Nothing big, just something to look over this week if you have the time. Think of it as therapeutic reading."

Why "this week"? Did she think I was coming back for round two? Did she expect it?

She removed a book from a shelf. The title mentioned something about happiness and feeling good. There was a photo of a woman on the cover. Her eyes were extra sparkly, and she looked ecstatic, in an "out-of-body experience" kind of way.

Elodie ended with an overall wrap-up and showed me out, handing over the book without asking for a second appointment. I didn't know what to make of it. Apparently she had more faith in me than I had in myself.

CHAPTER 36

"You have a visitor," Cade said when I entered his house. "She's in my office."

"Who is?"

Without waiting for a response, I rounded the corner. "Mrs. Bronson, what are you doing here?"

"Call me Lizzy. I was hoping we could talk, finish the conversation you started with my husband earlier."

"As much as I'd like your help, your husband made it clear he wasn't interested in what I had to say until I proved myself to him."

She took a seat, grinned at me like I was missing the point. "Who do you think sent me here?"

I sat across from her, thought about what she'd just said. "A few hours ago, your husband didn't want anything to do with me. What changed?"

She swished a hand through the air. "Politics. You know."

Actually, I didn't.

"Colt needs this case to go away, to be solved," she continued. "Hell, everyone does. Over the past week, he's received a handful of complaints from people in the community. Each day, the number grows. People here are outraged. They don't think we're doing enough to find the child."

"He's the mayor. He'll never please everyone, as I'm sure you know."

"Our goal is to keep people happy, make them feel safe and content, in their homes and in this valley. Colt plans to run for reelection, and something like this ... well, let's just say we don't need it to resurface again come election time in a way that tarnishes his reputation."

"I understand."

"I don't think you do," she said. "We can manage the backlash now, but things like this always get resurrected when there's a formidable opponent involved. And let's just say the man who's gearing up to run against my husband only knows how to play ball one way. He'll use everything in his power to dirty the minds of the voters."

The longer she droned on, the more I felt her motive for being here was based more on political gain and less on Finn's recovery.

"Why are you telling *me* this instead of Chief Rollins? Seems he's quite chummy with your husband."

"Perception, Miss Monroe. It's important Colt keeps up appearances, shows he's doing everything he can, working with the chief as a united front." She paused a moment then said, "I have big plans for my husband. After his second term as mayor, he'll run for governor."

"And then what—the White House?"

"Well now, maybe you *do* understand."

It made sense to me why Mayor Bronson and Chief Rollins had met up earlier, no doubt to make it appear they were working together to bring Finn home. On one hand, they were. Of course they wanted the baby to be found. On the other, both had hidden agendas, personal reasons I didn't want to take part in.

"To be clear, Mrs. Bronson, I have no interest in assisting your husband with his political aspirations. That has nothing to do with why I've agreed to assist with this case."

"Don't you *know* why I'm here, why I've come to *you* about this? Over the past few years, Chief Rollins has started slipping up, forgetting things here and there, making the kind of errors a person in his position can't afford to make. Ask Cade. He's seen it. He knows. The chief doesn't *want* to retire. He's being *forced* to retire."

I felt like a teenage girl in a locker room, eavesdropping on secrets that weren't any of my business. "None of this matters to me."

"It should. We both want the same thing."

"I don't think we do. Regardless of your reasons for being here, I'll keep looking for Finn until I find him—with or without permission."

She looked at me in a way that made me question her devotion to her husband, upping my already amplified level of discomfort. "I like you, Sloane. You seem like a bold, daring woman. A woman not afraid to speak her mind. Even your stubborn sense of morality is refreshing."

Maybe because she didn't have any.

"I need to get home and tend to the baby," she said. "If you have questions for me, let's get started."

I wanted nothing more than to speed up her departure. But right now, she was the only lead I had. "The night you delivered, I heard it was congested on the maternity floor."

"There were those who felt we caused a commotion when our friends and family stopped by. A bunch of nonsense, if you ask me."

"Did you see Hannah while you were there, or anyone else hanging around her room?"

She shook her head. "My suite was at the end of the floor. Miss Kinkade's was several rooms away. We asked for the suite because it was the biggest and most private room they had. It was at the end of the hallway. From what we were told, our visitors were still loud enough to irritate one of the other mothers."

"Hannah?"

"Someone else. An angry, mean-spirited woman. Because of her outburst, many who came to see us were rudely turned away, forced to leave."

"Maybe the woman was trying to keep things quiet for her own baby, or herself, after she delivered."

"I don't care what her reasons were," she said. "It's a hospital, not a monastery. If she wanted complete silence, she should have hired a midwife and had her baby at home."

"Did you ever see the woman, or meet her?"

"I asked Colt to talk to her, calm her down. I knew once the woman recognized who he was, who *we* were, she'd shut her trap."

"And did he talk to her?"

"He decided to get me an early release instead. We had help waiting for us at home, so there was no reason to remain there any longer."

"Did you notice anyone hanging around? Anyone who wasn't there to see you?"

"If they weren't there to see us, no."

She stood.

"Don't give up now. Please. We're counting on you." She slipped an envelope into my hand, closed hers over it. "*I'm* counting on you. Find the child. Don't let me down."

After she walked out, I tore the seal on the envelope, pulled out a wad of hundred-dollar bills, fanned them across my hand like a deck of playing cards. When reality struck, I went after her. She was already gone.

"Whadd'ya have there?" Cade glanced at my money fan then at me.

"I … umm … Mrs. Bronson shoved an envelope into my hand as she was leaving. I'll stop by her house. Give it back to her."

"Keep it."

"What?"

"If you were back in Park City, this would be a job. Just because what you're doing involves my family doesn't mean you don't deserve to be compensated for it."

"That's what it means to me."

"It shouldn't. How much have you got there?"

I had no idea. Thousands. Maybe ten thousand. Maybe more.

"I didn't want to tell you this, but I was plannin' on payin' you myself whether you accepted it or not," he said.

"I would have never allowed you to, Cade."

"Let's make a deal then. I won't give you any money if you agree to keep what Lizzy gave you. You've earned it, and you deserve it. Besides, think of it this way—that family is drowning in money, and for once, I'm seeing it being used for good."

Whatever decision I made, it didn't have to be made right now. There was something a lot more important I needed to do, and it couldn't wait.

CHAPTER 37

Jack looked better. Not great. But better. His face no longer reflected the pallid hue I'd come to expect. When I arrived at Bonnie's house with Cade, Jack was out back, rocking back and forth on a swing. No coat, no sweater, dressed in short sleeves, khakis, and white socks pulled up as high as they would go. Seemed every resident in Wyoming had warm blood coursing through their veins.

"Mind if I sit with you?" I asked.

Jack scooted several inches to one side, flicked a couple fingers my way. "Not at all."

I ran my hands up and down my arms, yearning for a coat instead of an airy sweater. Cade entered his aunt's house, returned with a thick blanket, unfolded it over my body. He parked a chair in front of the swing, sat down.

"Anything new?" Jack asked.

"Nothin' promising yet," Cade said. "Sorry, Jack."

"I know you're trying." Jack looked at me. "I know you're both trying. It means everything to me."

"I was hoping to ask you a few questions," I said. "If you don't mind?"

He nodded. "Go ahead."

"The night you were at the hospital, besides Hannah, two other women also delivered, the mayor's wife and one other woman, correct?"

"As far as I know."

"I was told the hospital staff sent several of the mayor's visitors home."

A look of disgust expanded across his face. "Not soon enough. They were coming and going for hours before one of the docs worked up the nerve to put a stop to it. Visiting hours were long over. The mayor's wife didn't seem to care. The rules didn't apply to her. She found out her cousin was refused visitation and kicked up a fuss. Next thing I knew, I saw her entourage hauling all this baby stuff down the hall. One of the nurses told me she'd been discharged."

"I know you waited outside Hannah's room for a while before Finn was brought out. Did you see anyone who shouldn't have been there? Anyone just hanging out, poking around?"

"We were so keyed up about seeing our …"

He choked on the last few words, unable to get them out.

I ran a hand up his arm. "Jack, I don't want to upset you. If this is too hard—"

"If talking to me helps in some way, I don't care."

I imagined the scene in my mind—the night Hannah was in the hospital. I saw the mayor and his wife, their visitors. I saw Hannah in her room. Her aunt in the hall with Jack and Serena. Teresa. Nurses and other hospital staff coming and going. I put myself in my vision—thought about what I already knew about that night, and what I didn't. Thought about what holes hadn't been filled. What questions hadn't been asked.

"The other woman who gave birth," I said, "she was angry, right? She complained over the noise from the mayor's visitors."

Jack nodded. "She had every right to be upset."

"She'd just had a baby," I said. "I'm sure she just wanted to rest."

"There's more to it."

"What do you mean?" I asked.

"The woman wasn't upset because she'd just had a baby. I mean, she did have a baby, but she lost it."

"How do you know her baby died?"

"After Finn was born, I watched the nurse take him over to the nursery. I followed, watched him through the glass. Finally getting the chance to be a father after all this time, I didn't want to let him out of my sight. A woman walked up, stood beside me. When I looked at her, I noticed her eyes were swollen. She asked me which one of the babies was mine. I showed her, asked her which one was hers. She burst into tears and ran off."

"Did you see her again?"

"Her husband came up to me a few minutes later. He apologized, said they'd lost their baby not long after he was born."

"Do you know what happened? Do you know why their baby died?"

"He didn't say."

"Did either of them ever mention their names?" Cade asked.

Jack shook his head. "I saw them one other time, only for a few seconds when we were leaving the hospital with Finn. We passed by their room. The woman was in the hospital bed. It looked like she was asleep. The man was in the bed with her, his hand wrapped around her, head resting on her shoulder."

Jack leaned back, tugged on his chin, revisiting the moment in his mind.

"What is it?" Cade asked.

"You know what? There *was* someone else—a man standing in the hallway between our room and the woman's room who lost the baby. I assumed he was with the other family, since we'd never seen him before. Can't say for sure. I never saw him talk to anyone."

"When did you see him?"

"On our way out."

"Did you get a good look at him?"

Jack shook his head.

"He kept his head down. I can't even tell you his hair color. The hat he wore covered it up."

"What kind of hat?"

"Beanie. Had a camouflage design."

We pressed Jack for additional details. His recollection was slim, even physical descriptions proved onerous. First he thought the woman's hair was brown, then red. Her husband was around six feet tall, then he was taller. At the time, there had been no reason to pay them any mind. Now, he had every reason.

CHAPTER 38

I was tired, exhausted enough to actually have a fair shot at indulging in some decent sleep. As the lids of my eyes became more weighted, I strained to stay awake long enough to finish another passage in my grandfather's journal.

Difficult day today. One of the worst I've experienced in my new position in the FBI. I've been told by my fellow agents it's far from the worst thing I'll encounter over the years, although right now, I can't imagine anything as gruesome as this. For the last several weeks, we've been searching for an eighteen-year-old girl named Anna Davis who went missing after her shift at the local burger joint in Chicago.

We believe Miss Davis is the fourth young woman to disappear in the last two months. The other three victims, all women, all around the same age, had been recovered by local police in the area in which their bodies were found. All were tied up and strangled, their bodies dumped in a heavily wooded area along the interstate. Not buried, just left there like they were meant to be found, like he, the killer, is taunting us.

With no promising leads and a woman being found on average of once a week, we were called down to investigate. Anna Davis's body was discovered today bound in the same manner as the other victims, but it appears the killer's ritual is escalating, becoming more aggressive. Over seventy-five percent of Anna's body was bloodied and beaten. Combined with the elements she'd been left in, and the four days it took to find her, it was a messy, unforgettable sight.

I consider myself to be a tough man, a strong man, having never met anyone with the same level of fortitude I possess, but even I succumbed to a sickened state when I came upon her. And now, as I sit at my desk, watching the sun as it begins to rise, I'm left to wonder if we could have saved her if only we'd arrived a few days before. The very thought leaves me harrowed with guilt, strapped by anxiety, knowing the limited timeframe we have to find the killer before he strikes again. A day, two maybe. Not much more.

It's times like these when most men question their line of work. Not me. If anything it gives me the resolve to start each day stronger than the day before, knowing

I will go on, because I must go on, for the victims, for their families.

For every wrong in this world, there's a right, a day when justice is administered to the guilty, if not by my own hand, and if not in this life, then it's sure to be found in the next. To the fallen, the innocent victims of these horrendous crimes, I shed a tear, mourn each victim, each life. But I never allow myself to fall into despair. I simply cannot.

I closed the book feeling renewed, determined. I wasn't just anyone. I was a Monroe. My grandfather's flesh and blood, and I wouldn't let him down.

CHAPTER 39

I sat with Cade in the hospital parking lot the next morning with a list of vague physical descriptions in my hand that had been provided to me by Jack the night before. Aside from a couple doctors, there had been five additional members of staff on the maternity ward the night Hannah had Finn. Jack claimed he'd overheard one staff member counting down the hours until her shift change at eight a.m. Time to find out if the same work hours applied today.

Two women exited the building, playfully giggling with one another as they sauntered to their cars, which happened to be parked next to each other.

"What do you think?" Cade asked.

"Too risky. Looks like they'll follow each other out of the parking lot. We need to get one of them alone, away from the rest."

A few minutes later, another woman pushed the glass door open and stepped out. A man followed, exiting a few feet behind. The woman hunched over as she walked, her eyes darting around, paranoid, untrusting.

Cade glanced at the paper in my hand, then at the girl. "She doesn't match the description of any of the women Jack said were workin' that night. Even if she did, she'd likely pepper us with mace if we tried approachin' her."

I was only half listening. My attention had diverted to the next candidate, a young man in his early twenties, whistling as he strolled to his car. He was in no hurry. Neither was I. "This guy looks encouraging."

My vote of approval was enough for Cade. He prepared to exit the truck. I placed a hand on his arm.

"You're staying," I said.

"Correction. I'm going."

"If this guy recognizes you and tells someone Jackson Hole's next chief of police solicited him in the parking lot to betray the confidentially of a patient by revealing her name, you could lose everything before you have it. By sending me, you expose nothing."

"It's a risk I'm willing to—"

"Let me do this," I said. "Besides, he's a guy. I can get more out of him than you can."

No matter how much Cade wanted to disagree, he knew I was right. My charming side came out full throttle when pertinent information was at stake. One little break was all we needed.

I exited the vehicle, walked in the kid's direction. In the last several seconds, he'd taken a call and lengthened his stride. Another minute and he'd be gone.

"Hey," I called out. "Can I talk to you?"

The kid turned, looked at me, looked behind him like I was talking to someone else.

"Yes, you," I said. "Can we talk?"

"Do I know you?"

"You don't."

He raked a few fingers through his straggly, long hair, fished out a black elastic, allowed his wild mane to fly free.

"You work on the maternity ward, right?" I asked.

"Yeah. Why?"

"I was wondering if I could talk to you about the night Hannah Kinkade was here."

"Who?"

I was getting ahead of myself.

"Were you working the night the mayor's wife had her baby?" I asked.

He nodded. We were getting somewhere.

"There were two other woman who had babies that night, right?" I asked.

"Guess so."

"Do you remember one of the mother's throwing a fit over the noise caused by the mayor's visitors?"

"Yeah, the ginger. She was pissed."

"She lost her baby, didn't she?"

"Yeah."

"What happened?" I asked.

He braced his muscular body against his car, cocked his head to the side. "Why are you asking? What's it to you?"

"Have you heard about the missing baby—the one taken from here?"

"Who hasn't?"

"I'm trying to find him," I said.

He was unfazed. "You and everyone else."

By the way he kept jangling his keys in his hand, it was obvious his interest was waning. He had somewhere else to be.

"The ginger-haired woman—why did she lose her baby?" I asked. "I need to know. Please. It's important."

"Fifty."

"Excuse me?"

"You want answers, I want fifty bucks."

It seemed my newly acquired cash was already coming in handy. I jammed a hand inside my pocket, peeled back three twenties, stuck them inside his hand.

"Keep the change, now answer the question."

"It was a premature delivery."

"Due to what?"

"Guess they were hiking somewhere around here, and she fell. Not sure if that was the main cause of death though."

"How far along was she?"

"I dunno for sure. Around twenty-five weeks from what everyone was saying. I saw the little guy for a minute."

"The baby?"

He nodded.

"A boy. He weighed almost nothing when he came out. A pound maybe. Doctor tried to save him, but there was some kind of problem with his heart. He didn't last long."

"During your shift, did you see a man standing in the hall wearing a knit camouflage hat?"

"We were busy. Lots of people were coming and going that night."

It was a strong possibility the man would have been caught on at least one of the hospital's surveillance cameras. To view the footage, we'd need to work with the chief, tell him why my focus went in the opposite way his did. I wanted to explore one more alternative first. "I need the name of the woman who lost the baby."

"I don't know it. And even if I did, I couldn't give it to you. I could lose my job."

I dug back in my pocket, flashed a hundred-dollar bill in front of his face.

He waved his hands in the air in front of him. "Nope, can't do it."

His mouth said no, but his eyes locked on the Benjamin Franklin.

"I realize what I'm asking," I said. "If you can get me her name, I'll add another Benjamin."

He gulped a hefty breath of air.

"You're offering me two hundred dollars for one name?"

"That's right."

"Why do you need it so bad?"

"I can't say," I said. "You interested or not?"

"Let's say I am. What am I supposed to tell everyone when I walk back in there?"

"I'm sure you'll figure something out."

He hadn't committed one way or the other, and my patience was wearing thin. If the ginger woman didn't know the mysterious man in the hallway, we needed to get the chief involved, find out who the guy was, why he was there. "What's it going to take?"

He grinned, giving away his next play. If I had a few hundred in my pocket, I probably had more.

"Five hundred."

"Done," I said. "You give me the name, I give you the money. Fifteen minutes or the deal's off."

He took his time walking back inside the hospital. I considered whether he was actually sold on my proposal, and what would happen if he had a change of heart and turned on me instead. Once I could no longer see the guy, Cade put his truck in gear and drove over, even though I'd tried to message him to remain in place.

"I sent the kid back inside to get the name of the woman we need to find," I said.

He winked. "How much did it cost you?"

"It'll be worth it if we get what we need. You need to get out of here. He thinks I'm alone. I want to keep it that way."

Cade returned to his post, and I glanced at the time. Fourteen minutes had passed. Another two or three, and I'd have to assume the deal was off.

The kid returned to the parking lot with a monstrous grin on his face. "You got the money?"

I displayed the five bills.

He held out a hand.

I hesitated. "The name."

"Samantha Wilcox. And hey, I'm feeling generous."

"Meaning?"

"I'll give you something extra, free of charge. She doesn't live here."

"What do you mean?"

"I was thinking about it, and I remembered hearing something she said to her husband that night."

"Go on."

"She said they never should have come here—to Jackson. She said it was his fault they lost the baby."

"How did he respond?" I asked.

"He said it was her idea to visit Sage, not his."

Sage. I tucked the name away and handed him the money, pinching it between my thumb and forefinger before I let go. "If I find out you've lied to me, I'll be back."

He snickered like it was some kind of empty threat, looked at me like my slender physique didn't alarm him.

"Trust me," I said. "You don't want to see me again."

CHAPTER 40

If Samantha Wilcox was only visiting Jackson Hole with her husband when she went into labor unexpectedly, finding where she was staying and where she was from would involve a generous amount of digging. Digging I didn't have time for. I abandoned my search of her name for the time being and shifted my focus to Sage, believing Sage to be a woman. Or hoping she was one.

Cade surprised me by saying Sage could have been the name of a place, not the name of a person. A town named Purple Sage actually existed in Wyoming. Given the town was a three-hour drive from Jackson Hole and was inhabited by less than six hundred residents, it was only a remote possibility this was what her husband had been referring to. If Samantha had been in Purple Sage, she wouldn't drive to Jackson to deliver when other suitable hospitals were close by.

"Sage isn't a common name," I said.

Cade searched the name "Sage" and the name "Wilcox," separately and together. No match.

"What about a variation of the name?" I suggested.

"What are you thinkin'?"

"Maybe it's spelled another way. Try Saige, just the first name, no last name."

Bingo.

Saige Hamilton.

And the best part?

She lived less than ten miles away.

CHAPTER 41

Saige Hamilton's home was dated and small, but located inside a gated subdivision that had been divided into five-acre parcels. A pricy, white sedan was parked on the right side of the driveway. On the left side of the house, I noticed semi-dry, muddy tire tracks in two different sizes, and four square impressions left in the dirt. The tire tracks trailed all the way to the street.

"From the looks of these tracks, something was parked here recently," I said.

Cade crouched down, stared at the tracks, at the sunken square shapes in the dirt. "Trailer maybe. Judgin' by the distance, could be a fifth wheel."

No one came to the door when we knocked, and after waiting outside for a decent amount of time, impatience took hold. I tried the door handle. It wasn't locked.

"Hello? Saige Hamilton?" I pushed open the door, pausing before I walked inside. "Are you here?"

The only sound I heard was a faint hum coming from one of the appliances in the kitchen. Glancing around the neighborhood, the houses were a short distance from one another, but not so far off a neighbor couldn't be watching. I saw no one outside, no prying eyes. In my experience, that didn't mean we didn't have gawkers.

"What do you think?" I asked.

"Do it. Go in."

The two of us stepped into a living room. It was immaculate, decorated with a sofa and a high-back chair. Both white. Both in the kind of pristine condition that said no one actually used this room much, if at all. The furniture was for show. Not a single item was out of place. Not a glass, a remote control, nothing. Even the pillows on the couch were plumped to perfection, lined out next to each other, each the same width apart, like they'd been individually placed with great care.

The kitchen was a different story. While a stellar example of cleaning at its finest, I spied a half-empty baby bottle tipped over inside the sink and sprinkles of what I first thought was salt all over the counter. At second glance, the granules were fine, like powdered milk.

"Look at this," I said.

Cade's eyes followed my finger to the sink. "You would think if this woman had a baby, there'd be a high chair in this room, a swing in the other."

"You'd also think white furniture would be out of the question."

I opened the cabinets, found nothing but stacks of adult-sized dishes, cups. Nothing out of the ordinary. Nothing else belonging to a baby. I tried the refrigerator. Same result.

Sitting on the counter in a wicker basket was a set of keys and a wallet. I snapped the clasp on the front of the wallet open, pulled out a driver's license belonging to a red-headed Saige Hamilton. The other four pockets in the wallet were lined with credit cards. If she wasn't home, why leave her wallet behind? Her home was miles from the nearest store, so the only answer I could come up with was either she *was* there, or she'd walked to a neighbor's house.

"Let's check the rest of the house," Cade said.

Photos of Saige lined both sides of the wall in the hallway. In the pictures, Saige was engaged in various activities—skiing, climbing, dining at an elegant restaurant, steering a sailboat on the ocean. The collage was devoid of children and men. In fact, Saige was the only person in every photo except one. I lifted the anomaly off the wall. Saige had her arm draped around another redhead. I recognized the location the photo was taken, in front of the antler arch in Town Square.

"This could be Samantha," I said to Cade. "If it is, they look almost identical, which would make them sisters."

I skimmed the other photos as I continued down the hall, until my eyes noticed something else, a smeared streak on the wall. In an unsullied house like this one, it stood out. I flipped on the hall light, bent down, looked closer.

Cade crouched down next to me. "What have you found?"

"This looks like dried blood."

He bolted back to a standing position, bobbed his head inside one of the two rooms at the end of the hallway, found nothing. He stopped inside the doorway of the second room. I watched his eyes close, his chest rise and fall. I didn't even need to ask. I'd seen the same look before. I knew what he'd seen.

CHAPTER 42

Saige Hamilton was laying on her left side on the floor, her body coiled like the folds in an accordion. She'd taken a single bullet, as noted by the entry wound on the side of her forehead.

The site wasn't neat and tidy this time. Blood was on the wall, the furniture, all over the carpet. The blood on the wall probably started as spatter until someone made an attempt to clean it. Red swirl patterns circled the wall in front of me, indicating someone started soaking up the mess. Why then hadn't they finished? The sloppy cleanup job was half-assed, like the person had been interrupted, or perhaps they'd been stopped, forced to leave the half-wiped, blood-spattered room behind.

Saige's hands and feet were bluish in color, her lips pale. Rigor mortis had begun, affecting her eyelids, neck, and jaw. It hadn't spread throughout her body yet, meaning her death had been recent. How recent we wouldn't know until the coroner arrived.

A cell phone rested a few inches from Saige's body. It was an older model flip phone. And it was open. Had she tried to reach out to someone right before she was murdered? Or had the call itself been the reason for her murder? I wanted to grab it, look up her last call. Most of the time, I'd take a gamble. This time, Cade had already called in reinforcements, forcing me to play by the rules. Most of them anyway.

"It looks to me like whoever did this knocked her around first."

I eyeballed the presumptuous male officer poised behind me. He was young, so young he couldn't have been a cop for long. I wondered what someone so fresh and unaware was doing here, and why he wasn't with his partner.

"She wasn't beaten," I said.

"How do you explain the discoloration then?"

"Lividity."

I waited for him to ask me what the word *lividity* meant. He didn't. Instead, he got down on all fours, aligning his face so close to Saige's, I shuddered. Dead bodies made me squeamish. This kid seemed fascinated.

"Don't touch her," I said. "She hasn't been examined yet."

Upon hearing my reprimand, he grimaced. "Wasn't going to, miss."

He propped his body back up to a kneeling position, stuck a hand out. I took it.

"Where's your partner?" I asked.

"I'm Nash Crawford."

He dodged the partner question and introduced himself by his first name instead of Officer Crawford. Strange. "Sloane Monroe."

"Haven't seen you around here before."

"I'm here with Cade."

"Detective McCoy?"

I nodded.

"Oh."

His response, while simple, carried a sort of admiration and esteem with it, like he revered Cade. I didn't blame him.

"I take it this is your first dead body?" I asked.

"Is it that obvious?"

"Just an observation."

He fussed with the collar on his shirt. "This kind of thing doesn't happen a lot around here. From looking at her, I assumed this was a domestic dispute. What do you think?"

For a novice, he was eager to learn.

"The discoloration you see on her arm and leg are natural given her body's position," I said.

"How so?"

"When a person dies, their heart stops beating, as you already know. When the heart fails to pump, blood stops flowing. This is what it looks like when the blood settles. It may look like abuse, but it's not."

"Impressive." Hooker entered the room with Cade. "Would you like to do the autopsy for me too while you're here?"

Hooker laughed. I didn't. Not because I didn't appreciate his attempt to amuse me, but because Chief Rollins entered the room behind him, face solemn. For the moment, he ignored me, concentrated on the kid still knelt next to Saige.

"Nash, what are you doing here?"

The kid stared at the ground, his face pale.

"I … umm … heard about it on the radio and decided to come over, take a look."

"You can't be here. You could have contaminated the scene."

"Sorry, Grandpa. I just wanted to check it out, you know? I'm a cop now. Can't I do that?"

Grandpa?

"He didn't touch anything," I said. "I made sure of it."

Without facing me, Chief Rollins said, "*You* shouldn't be here either."

"You're here *because* I'm here, because Cade and I found this place."

He didn't respond. Instead, he grabbed Nash by the arm and escorted him out of the room.

"Nice kid," I said to Cade. "He perked right up when I mentioned your name."

Cade grimaced. "He has a thing for Shelby. Been comin' around the house a lot lately."

"And you don't approve?"

"He's four years older than she is, and you just saw who he has for a grandfather."

I suppose at Shelby's age, four years was a big deal. Still, I didn't see why it mattered. Our conversation halted when Hooker went to work on the body, first making a small incision into Saige's abdomen, inserting a thermometer into her liver tissue. I turned away, unable to watch.

"I'm trying to get her—"

"Core body temperature," I said, remaining turned around. "I know."

"Well, aren't you full of surprises," Hooker said.

"You're not the only medical examiner she knows," Cade said. "Not the best lookin' either."

I backed out of the room as the rest of Hooker's team arrived to process the scene. While the medical experts did their job, investigators dissected the house. Cade and Hooker talked, giving me the opportunity to slip out. I walked to the house next door. No one was home. I tried the next house. Same result. As I started up the driveway to the third house, I was met by the kind of couple that looked like they could have passed for brother and sister, even though they were probably husband and wife. Their eyes were glazed over, fascinated with the cars gathered at the end of the street.

"What's goin' on over there?" the woman asked. "We walked over, tried to find out what was happening. They told us a whole lot of nothin' and sent us back home."

"I can't say just yet."

"Oh, come on. Please," the woman begged. "We have a bet going, and I'm sure I'm right."

A bet. People never ceased to amaze me. Neighborly sentimentality aside, they were eager, exactly the kind of people I hoped to find.

"How well do you know Saige Hamilton?" I asked.

The woman responded first. "Not well at all. She's lived there a year, and we've only spoken a couple times. Keeps to herself, that one."

"She's friendly to me," the man added. "She smiles and waves whenever she drives by."

The woman pressed her hands to her hips. "How nice for you. She doesn't wave to *me*."

"Did she have a camper parked next to her house?" I asked.

"Ugliest thing you've ever set eyes on," the woman said. "I left a note on her door complainin' about it. She didn't do a thing. Didn't even bother comin' over here to talk to me about it."

"How long has it been there?"

"Twelve days."

"Did the camper belong to Saige?"

The woman shook her head. "A man."

"What can you tell me about him?"

"He just showed up one day in that unsightly piece of trash, parked it on the side of the house, and moved in."

"Now, honey," the man said. "We're not sure if he moved in. We don't even know who he is. He could have been visiting for all we know."

"So neither of you ever talked to the guy?"

They shook their heads in unison.

"The camper's gone. When did that happen?"

"Today," the man said. "About two hours ago."

"No, not that long," the woman said. "It's only been about an hour. I know because I was watching *The View* when it passed by."

The man rolled his eyes. The woman smiled, leaned in close. "If you tell me why all these police have invaded our street, I'll make it worth your while."

"Fine," I said. "Tell me what you know."

"Oh no. I know how this works. I tell you somethin', and you don't tell me anything. I don't think so."

If it was anyone else, I might have hesitated, but town gossips thrived on two things: attention and keeping up on the latest information.

"The police are here investigating the death of Saige Hamilton."

The woman's head started bobbing around in a kind of spastic motion. "I knew it! I just knew someone was dead!"

Without saying another word, she ran inside her house and closed the door.

"Is she coming back, do you think?"

The man laughed. "She lives for this kind of drama. Give her an hour, and she'll have found a way to spin the story into something that involves her directly. She'll have all her friends believing it too."

"Don't you be spreadin' lies about me, Stu." The woman returned, paper in hand.

"What's this?"

"The license plate from the truck pullin' the camper."

I felt like she'd just placed a sizable gold nugget in my hand.

The man shook his head. "What on earth is wrong with you?"

"I told you somethin' was off about that man," the woman replied. "And I was right."

"When the man left, was he alone?" I asked.

"Oh no. There were four of them, all left together. The man with the camper, another man, a woman, and a baby."

CHAPTER 43

"The truck is registered to a Derrick Hamilton from Lyman, Wyoming, and the car out front is registered to Samantha Wilcox."

Derrick Hamilton was identified as Saige and Samantha's brother. He was also a convicted felon, a thief, having served a short time in jail for armed robbery. Had he just added baby snatcher to his rap sheet?

"Lyman?"

What a funny name.

"It's a small town a few hours from here."

The chief put in a call to the Lyman Police Department. Two officers were sent to Derrick's residence to watch and wait, should Derrick make a false move and head for home. An APB was also issued.

Saige's body was loaded up, transported to the lab for further analysis. From what Hooker had already observed, she hadn't been dead long. After the initial tests, he narrowed the timeline down to the last few hours. The neighbor was certain she'd seen the camper pull out only an hour before, which meant after the murder, the killer, or killers, stuck around for a while. Now they were running scared, trying to decide their next move.

We were on the right track. I was sure of it. A baby bottle had been found in the house of a person who had no baby. There was a connection between the Wilcox and the Westwood families, both of them present at the hospital on the same day. Derrick and Saige were Samantha's sister and brother. And, another dead body had been found, similar to the way Serena's was before.

"I can't stand this," I said to Cade. "The waiting. I need to be out there doing something."

"If this guy has Finn, he'd be an idiot to return to his house now."

I wasn't so sure. Idiocy seemed to be a growing pandemic.

"He's hauling a trailer. Even if they left over an hour ago, the trailer will most likely slow them down."

"If he's headed toward Lyman, there are two main routes he could take—through Green River or Evanston."

Out of the corner of my eye, I watched Chief Rollins exit Saige's house. He was talking to one of the investigators while keeping tabs on Cade, like he planned to come our way next.

"Do you think Derrick is headed back to his hometown?" I asked.

Cade tugged at the sleeve of my shirt, tipped his head toward his truck. "Only one way to find out."

CHAPTER 44

Knowing there were several officers patrolling both stretches of highway, we elected to try something different. Although the drive wasn't much more than miles and miles of uninhabited land, there were a few towns here and there, gas stations, a couple diners even. We banked on the fact Derrick would make a stop somewhere.

We drove over an hour and didn't meet anyone who claimed to have seen the truck, the trailer, or its inhabitants. The chief called once, then a second time. I assumed by now he knew where we'd gone. I also assumed he wasn't happy. I didn't care. He'd sanctioned our help. Too late now.

A skinny, boxcar-shaped, metallic building on the right side of the road caught my eye for two reasons. One, there was nothing but barren land for miles around, and two, because of the cosmic-looking sign out front that displayed the diner's name: Galaxy Burger. It looked like one of those restaurants from the fifties where waitresses rolled up to your car on skates, wearing silly hats on their heads and multi-layered, polka-dotted skirts with the ruffle peeking out of the hem.

"I got this one," I said.

I hopped out of the truck and took a couple steps toward the door, when something else caught my eye. A silver truck hitched to a long, beat-up trailer. I told myself to remain calm, not to overreact, but every body movement I made seemed tense, awkward, obvious.

Cade lowered the passenger-side window. "What's goin' on?"

I leaned inside the window, tried to act casual, like I'd forgotten to tell him something. When I tried to speak, I choked on my words at first, then managed to get out a simple fragment, "Trailer behind diner."

My instinct said to turn, glare through the windows of the diner, size up all of its patrons. I didn't dare. If they *were* inside, there was a good chance they were paranoid, watching every car, every person to arrive.

"Sloane, take a breath, go inside, and ask to use the restroom. Ask for a menu, pretend to order somethin' if you have to. You may have been spotted gettin' out of the truck, so it has to be you."

I wanted it to be me. I just didn't want to blow our cover.

The walk to the café entrance felt like five times the distance it should have. I kept my focus on the front door, tried not to gawk through the windows, tried to quiet my nerves. A few more steps and I'd be inside.

A "Please Seat Yourself" sign greeted me at the entrance. I looked up, tried to find a sign directing me to the restroom. I didn't see one. One of the female waitresses passed me, grazing my shoulder with the steaming pot of coffee she'd hoisted in one of her hands.

"Oh my goodness," she said. "I'm so sorry. Did that get you?"

"Do you have a restroom?"

"Sure, sweetie."

I was hoping she'd point to the aisle running left to right, so I could scope out one section walking to the restroom, and the other when I came out. She didn't. She aimed a finger straight ahead.

I walked to the restroom, entered, stood inside one of the stalls for a minute, walked back out. I craned my head around like I was searching for an empty table to sit at. In the process, I didn't see anyone matching the mug shot Cade showed me of Derrick Hamilton, didn't hear or see any babies. The booths were extra high, and extra padded, handicapping me from a full line of sight. Maybe I was wrong. Maybe they weren't here.

"Can I get you something?"

The waitress was back, sans the coffee pot, pen and pad in hand.

"Uh … coffee? To go."

I didn't drink coffee.

"Got it. Anything else? Pastry, slice of our delicious seven-layer chocolate cake for the road?"

I ordered the seven layers. The waitress trotted off to the kitchen. She pushed her way through a thin, reflective door. When it swayed closed, I caught a glimpse of something in its mirrored reflection. A camouflaged beanie hat.

CHAPTER 45

I handed Cade a full plate of cake, a fork, and a cup of coffee. "Derrick's in there. At least, I think he is."

"I ran the plates on the camper," Cade said. "It's his."

"There's a man sitting in a booth just behind the door to the kitchen. He's wearing the same kind of camouflage beanie hat Jack described. I didn't get a good look at his face. His back was to me, and he kept his head down. If it's him, we have a problem."

"Which is?"

"He's not sitting with anyone. He's alone. No baby. No sister. No brother-in-law."

"Huh." Cade crouched down in the seat, picked his phone out of his pocket. "Callin' the chief. We need back up."

Cade might have felt obligated to wait. I didn't. I opened Cade's center console, removed a hunting knife I'd noticed before, released it inside my jacket pocket.

"Now hang on, Sloane. Don't go back into the restaurant—"

The rest of his sentence trailed off in garbled, indistinguishable puff of air as I headed to the camper alone. I turned just long enough to see Cade frantically dialing the phone. I understood his need to follow protocol as much as I understood my own need not to.

I slashed both of Derrick's front tires when I reached his truck. As I removed the heavy, serrated blade from the second tire, I heard it. A sound coming from inside the camper. A baby. Crying. The sweet sound of discontent stirred every emotion from within my body.

I'd done it.

We'd done it.

We'd saved him.

Please, let it be him.

A second sound, footsteps, approached from behind. I whipped around, pointed my gun.

"Good hell, woman," Cade whispered. "Don't aim that thing at me."

"Don't rush me like that."

"Don't take off on me again."

I was too nervous to think of another comeback.

Cade assessed the flattened front tires. "I thought you could use my help. Looks like you've got it under control."

Tears clouded my eyes. I held them back. There would be time for all that later. My job, *our* job, wasn't finished yet.

"Do you hear that? Do you hear him? It's Finn, Cade. It has to be."

"I hear it, Sloane. Check inside the camper. I'll wait here."

I released the latch on the camper door, ascended the steps, gun extended. The crying stopped. Two people sat back to back on the ground in the far corner, a man and a woman, mouths gagged with a black cloth, hands bound with rope. Rope had also been wound around both of their bodies then secured to a long, metal rod under the sofa, leaving them incapable of any movement, any potential to escape. Aside from being bound, the woman looked unscathed. The man's shirt was soaked in blood, concealed by a jacket which had probably been used to smuggle him out of Saige's house without alarming the neighbors.

I approached the woman first, tugged the gag out of her mouth, stooped down. "Where's the baby?"

The woman blinked, paused, then said, "Please … help us. You don't know what he's—."

"If you want my help, tell me where the baby's at. Where's Finn?"

"You don't have time to—"

I brandished my gun, aimed it in her direction. She was right, there wasn't time. "The baby."

She bent her head forward. "In there."

"In there" was a small bathroom. Not seeing a child when I first walked in, I detected movement coming from the other side of a murky shower door. I opened it and looked down, looked at the mass of chocolate-colored hair, the beady eyeballs staring up at me, staring like he knew why I was there, knew I'd come to save him.

"Hi there." I holstered my gun, leaned down, unbuckled the car seat, placed a hand behind his head as I lifted him toward me. His delicate fingers clutched one of mine, and I thought of Hannah, realizing to a fuller extent how impossible it was for her to give up this precious baby.

"Find Finn?" Cade called from outside.

"I have him."

I stepped out, turned to the woman. "Samantha Wilcox?"

She nodded.

I shifted my gaze to the man beside her. "This your husband?"

"No."

What did she mean, *no?*

"If he isn't your husband, who is he?"

"He's … my brother."

CHAPTER 46

"The man in the restaurant isn't Derrick Hamilton," I yelled to Cade.

"Who is he then?"

The woman answered. "My husband, Rob. He has a gun."

"Sloane, stay where you are," Cade cautioned. "Stay with the baby."

Keeping Finn safe was foremost on my mind, and right now, Cade's intentions were right—the camper wasn't going anywhere. Minutes passed. Rob hadn't left the diner. Had he seen us? Bailed on foot? As long as he hadn't observed us going around the side of the building, it was just a matter of minutes, seconds even, before he appeared.

"Please, let us go," Samantha pleaded.

"Not until I know how you ended up with Jack and Serena's baby."

"There's no time. Rob could be back any minute."

"Give me the short version."

Samantha explained she'd lost herself after losing her baby, becoming swallowed up in her grief. Her husband, Rob, tried taking her back home. She refused to go. She wanted to be with her sister, her brother, her family. Not him. The days passed, each more difficult than the one before. Samantha distanced herself from her husband, refusing to speak to him.

"I told him I wanted a divorce," she said. "I told him my life would never be the same again after losing our son."

"What did he do?"

"He left. I thought he went home without me. A few days later he returned to my sister's house with a baby."

"Did you ask where the baby came from?"

"Of course I did. He said the child's mother overdosed on drugs. The baby had just been put into foster care. He said he filled out the paperwork, and they just handed him the baby. He thought trading our child for this one would fix things between us. Somehow he convinced himself this new baby would make everything better."

"Did you believe his story?"

"I'm no idiot. I'd seen the AMBER Alert on TV. Seen the baby's picture. So had Saige. I told him I knew he'd stolen the baby, killed the baby's mother, the same woman I saw at the hospital. Made me sick, what he'd done. You wanna know what he said? His only response was that the baby's mother wasn't a mother at all. She'd adopted the boy. Like that justified his actions somehow."

"You're saying he knew you disapproved and decided to hold you, your brother, and your sister hostage for several days?"

Seemed peculiar that three people could remain under Rob's eye for so long.

"Not my brother. Before Rob showed up, Derrick had taken the camper and went hiking in Yellowstone for a few days. He had no idea what was going on until he returned."

"I'm guessing that's when things got crazy," I said.

"Rob admitted to all of us what he'd done, thinking my brother would be on his side. He said he'd kept the kid himself for a few days after he took him while he worked up the nerve to bring him over. He thought he'd swoop in, win me over, and convince me to leave with him. He'd cleared both of our bank accounts and booked one-way tickets to Canada. Truth be told, he's never been very smart. I just never thought he was a killer."

"How did your sister die?"

"When Derrick came back, saw we were being held at gunpoint, saw the baby, he came up with a plan to distract Rob while Saige called the police. Rob followed her into the bedroom. As soon as she grabbed her phone and started to dial, he fired. Derrick ran in, and Rob turned, shot him too."

Feeling confident in her story, I removed the gag from Derrick's mouth. "Is what she's saying true?"

"Every word."

Outside I heard Cade yell, "Stop! Hands on your head. Right now! Don't move. I said don't … move!"

And then a gunshot went off.

CHAPTER 47

Rob Wilcox *had* moved, just not in the way Cade expected. Feeling defeated, and with no place left to go, Rob had lifted the gun to his own head, firing one last shot. He was dead. It was all over. I left Samantha and Derrick roped together until the police arrived to verify their story. I was sure everything Samantha told me was true, but now it was time to let the law take over. I had a beautiful bundle of joy to look after.

Once Finn's identity was confirmed, Cade asked the chief's permission for us to escort Finn back to Jack. I expected a resounding no, but since I was the only woman around, and hadn't let go of the child since I'd swaddled him in my arms, the chief let common sense be his guide.

I strapped Finn back into his car seat, hopped into the back seat with him, and closed the door.

"I saved him, Hannah," I whispered. "I did it. He's safe now."

Cade started the engine. "What's that?"

"Oh, nothing."

"I'm proud of you."

I buried my head in my hands, and wept.

I wept because I had lost Hannah.

I wept because I'd saved Finn.

I wept because I'd never had any children of my own.

I wept because I'd allowed myself to become lost, forsaking what mattered most.

I wept because my grandfather had been right about me all along.

The present, the past. It poured out of me like a dam finally seizing the opportunity to break. And I couldn't hold it inside any longer.

"I'm sorry," I said. "I don't know why I'm falling apart like this."

"Don't be." Cade reached back, cupped my chin in his hand, lifted my head so I faced him. "It's nice to finally meet you. The real you."

CHAPTER 48

Jack's front lawn looked like the main attraction at a family reunion when we arrived. I recognized many faces from Serena's funeral. Jack weaved through the crowd, opened the door. I got out and backed up, allowing him the chance to reach over, remove Finn. He didn't. Instead he spread his arms out, pulled me close. "Thank you. Thank you, and thank Cade for getting Serena the justice she deserves. She can finally be at rest. I'll never forget what the two of you have done. Never."

The next several hours passed in a joyous celebration. Many tears were shed for Serena, and a healthy dose of laughter spread through the crowd prompted by the return of Finn. After it died down, and only Jack's closest family lingered, a familiar car pulled up. Renee. I met her at the front door.

"I heard you found him," she said.

"We did."

"Can I come in?"

Jack approached from behind, Finn in hand. "Renee. Thanks for coming."

"Thanks for calling me, Jack. I never expected it."

"Would you like to hold him?" Jack asked.

I backed away, gave Renee the space she needed.

"It was nice of you to call her," I said. "After losing Hannah, and what she went through with her brother and his wife, I'm sure it means more to her than you know."

"Oh, I believe I do know," he said.

After Renee spent time with Finn, she passed him to Bonnie, and I watched Jack and Renee slip away together. When they returned, Jack said, "I've been doing some thinking the last few days. I just talked to Renee for a while, and uhh … I believe we have come to an agreement."

Bonnie raised a brow. "What kind of agreement?"

"I've given it a lot of thought, and, I'm not sure I'm the right person to raise Finn," Jack said. "If Serena was here, believe me, I'd feel different. She isn't here, and, the truth is, it's not the same raising him without her."

"You don't need Serena here to be a great father," Bonnie said.

"It's not that, Mom. I can't even take care of myself right now, let alone a newborn baby."

"You've got your family, your sister, me. We're all here for you. You won't raise him alone."

"I loved him from the moment I first saw him. Even though we only had him for a few weeks, he's still my son. In ways, he always will be. In other ways, I realize he also has a connection to Renee. When I first met Renee at the hospital, I could tell she wished she could raise Finn herself. She couldn't then. She can now. I don't feel right keeping him from her. I *won't* keep him from her."

"What are you sayin'?" Cade asked.

"If the state will allow it, and I believe they will, Renee is going to adopt Finn."

Bonnie smacked a hand over her mouth. "No, Jack. Please."

"This is what I've decided to do, Mom. I've had a lot of time to consider what's best for him. With Serena gone, I know in my heart this is right."

"Don't worry," Renee said. "Any of you. I'll never keep Finn from you. That's not my intention. I believe there's a way we can do this together, a way we can all be family, bonded together through our love for this little boy."

"Son, are you sure this is what you really want?" Bonnie asked. "Are you absolutely sure?"

He nodded.

"I am."

Although it was clear Bonnie had mixed feelings, I knew she wouldn't stand in his way. Renee and Jack shared a common bond—with Finn and in their grief. Bonnie was smart enough to know what it meant. She reached out, snatched Renee's hand, did her best to form a smile. "Well, Renee. Welcome to the family."

CHAPTER 49

I woke early, having slept a full, uninterrupted five hours the night before. It wasn't much, but it was a start. What began as a short weekend getaway had turned into one of the longest weekends of my life. I had bittersweet thoughts about heading for home.

Home.

Was it really?

Did I even belong there?

I had an open invitation from my grandmother to stay in her condo in Florida anytime I wanted for as long as I wanted. She was hardly ever there, and when she was, it wasn't for long. Somehow Florida didn't seem right either.

I stuffed the last of my toiletries into the front compartment of my suitcase and rolled it into the hallway. A teary-eyed Shelby was waiting, hands shoved inside her pockets, face inspecting the ground.

"Why the tears?" I asked. "I thought you'd be happy to see me go. I've taken far too much time away from you and your dad. Now you can have him all to yourself."

My attempt to make light of the situation fell flatter than a single sheet of paper.

"Yeah, I guess."

"Hey, look at me," I said. "It's not like I'm never coming back. Once I figure out where I'm going and what I'm doing, you can come stay with me anytime."

"I just thought …"

"Thought what?"

"Nothing. It's stupid."

"It isn't to me."

Cade entered the room. "You all packed then?"

I was standing in front of him with a zipped suitcase and keys in my hand, wondering when the awkwardness would end.

"Dad … say something," Shelby said.

"What do you want me to say?"

"You *know* what to say. Please. Don't let her leave."

"Sloane knows what's best for her right now, Shelby. We have to respect what she's decided. She stayed a lot longer than she planned."

"You don't want her to leave either. Tell her, Dad."

"I'll visit soon," I said. "I promise."

I tried to slip an arm around her back. She shrugged me off. I didn't push it. Cade seized the opportunity to sweep me up in his arms while a disgruntled Shelby stood against the wall, watching us like we couldn't be acting any more ridiculous. I wanted to pretend I didn't fully comprehend what was happening, even though every part of me did.

"Drive safe," he said. "Let me know when you get back. Okay?"

Drive safe. Let me know when you get back? That's it?

When had the man who confessed his love a few nights before made the decision to replace his charming, effervescent words with diplomacy? And why did I care? This was my choice, what I wanted, what I asked for—space, time.

I pulled back from his embrace and dished back what he'd served, thanking him for everything he'd done for me the past week, asking him to say goodbye to his family. Before I headed to the car, I turned, hoping I'd get one more chance to address Shelby. She was already gone.

"Should I go talk to her?" I asked. "I feel terrible. I don't want to leave knowing she's hurting because of me."

"She'll be fine. Give her a day or two. I'm sure she'll get over it."

He tried to sound convincing, but even he didn't seem to believe his words.

When I reached the driveway, Cade remained in the doorway, one hand stuffed inside his pocket, eyes glued to me. Why couldn't he just go back inside, close the door, make it easier for both of us?

I placed my bag in the back seat and stood there, my hands pressed against the roof of the car. My heart pounded inside my chest. Why didn't I feel better about leaving?

I spoke without turning around. "You're just going to stand there and let me leave? There's nothing else you want to say? Nothing at all?"

"Dammit, woman. You're impossible. I told you, if you wanna be part of my life you have to …"

He was behind me, standing so close I could feel the heat of his breath caressing my ear. For a moment we stood there, neither one of us relenting. Him wanting me to come to him. Me wanting him to come to me. The difference was … he *had* come to me before. And I'd done nothing.

"Say something," he whispered. "Talk to me."

I didn't say something, I *did* something. I flipped around, looped my arms around his neck and pulled him toward me, pressing my lips on his. He returned my kiss with one of his own, holding me close, not wanting to let go.

"I'm still figuring things out, Cade, but I know one thing—I'm not ready to leave."

"Don't then. Stay with me. Figure out what you really want."

I leaned against him, savoring the moment.

In the distance, I almost thought I saw a white horse.

THE END

All of Cheryl Bradshaw's novels are heavily researched, proofed, edited, and professionally formatted by a skilled team of professionals. Should you find any errors, please contact the author directly. Her assistant will forward the issue(s) to the publisher. It's our goal to present you with the best possible reading experience, and we appreciate your help in making that happen. You can contact the author through her website. http://www.cherylbradshaw.com/.

About Cheryl Bradshaw

Cheryl Bradshaw is a *New York Times* and *USA Today* bestselling author. She currently has two series: Sloane Monroe mystery/thriller series and the Addison Lockhart paranormal suspense series. Stranger in Town (Sloane Monroe series #4) was a 2013 Shamus Award finalist for Best PI Novel of the Year, and I Have a Secret (Sloane Monroe series #3) was a 2013 eFestival of Words winner for best thriller novel. To learn more:

Website: cherylbradshaw.com
Facebook: Cheryl Bradshaw Books
Twitter: @cherylbradshaw
Blog: cherylbradshawbooks.blogspot.com

And sign up for my quarterly author newsletter on my blog.

Enjoy the Story?

If you enjoyed *Hush Now Baby*, you can show your appreciation by leaving a review on Amazon, Barnes & Noble, iBooks, or in the Kobo Store. Cheryl is always grateful when a reader takes time out of their day to comment on my novels.

If you do write a review, please be sure email Cheryl at cherylbradshawbooks@yahoo.com so she can express her gratitude.

Books by Cheryl Bradshaw

Sloane Monroe Series
Black Diamond Death
Murder in Mind
I Have a Secret
Stranger in Town
Bed of Bones
Hush Now Baby

Addison Lockhart Series
Grayson Manor Haunting

Till Death do us Part Short Story Series
Whispers of Murder
Echoes of Murder (Coming Soon!)

Boxed Sets
Sloane Monroe Series (Books 1–3)
Sloane Monroe Series (Books 4–5)

Made in the USA
Middletown, DE
29 December 2014